Prologue

START READING!

A while ago, when I was younger and kind of knock-kneed, I attended the Alton School for the Remarkably Giftless. None of the students seemed to have a single gift. In music class, our kazoos honked like a flock of injured geese. In art class, we drew only stick figures. In gym class, dodge ball was called air ball and not much fun at all – no one could dodge a ball, but no one could really throw one either so it didn't matter. Even the bullies were giftless. They didn't know how to give nuggies. Their spitballs were too dry. And they always bungled their wedgies. Sometimes I'd give them my lunch money just because they'd look all teary-eyed and I felt so sorry for them.

Basically, we were a shuffly, sloppy, sad little crew of children.

THE AMAZING COMPENDIUM of EDWARD MAGORIUM

—AS TOLD TO N. E. BODE—

PUFFIN

PUFFIN BOOKS

Published by the Penguin Group
Penguin Books Ltd, 80 Strand, London WC2R 0RL, England
Penguin Group (USA) Inc., 375 Hudson Street, New York, New York 10014, USA
Penguin Group (Canada), 90 Eglinton Avenue East, Suite 700, Toronto, Ontario, Canada M4P 2Y3
(a division of Pearson Penguin Canada Inc.)
Penguin Ireland, 25 St Stephen's Green, Dublin 2, Ireland (a division of Penguin Books Ltd)
Penguin Group (Australia), 250 Camberwell Road, Camberwell, Victoria 3124, Australia
(a division of Pearson Australia Group Pty Ltd)
Penguin Books India Pvt Ltd, 11 Community Centre, Panchsheel Park, New Delhi – 110 017, India
Penguin Group (NZ), 67 Apollo Drive, Rosedale, North Shore 0632, New Zealand
(a division of Pearson New Zealand Ltd)
Penguin Books (South Africa) (Pty) Ltd, 24 Sturdee Avenue, Rosebank,
Johannesburg 2196, South Africa

Penguin Books Ltd, Registered Offices: 80 Strand, London WC2R 0RL, England

puffinbooks.com

First published in the USA by Scholastic Inc. in cooperation with Walden Media, LLC, 2007
Published in Great Britain in Puffin Books 2007

1

Artwork copyright © 2007 Walden Media, LLC. All rights reserved.
Photos copyright © 2007 Stupid Zebra, LLC. All rights reserved.
Copyright © 2007 Stupid Zebra, LLC. All rights reserved.

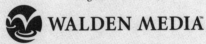

Walden Media and the Walden Media skipping stone logo are trademarks and registered trademarks
of Walden Media, LLC, 294 Washington Street, Boston, Massachusetts 02108, USA

Set in Hoefler Text
Made and printed in England by Clays Ltd, St Ives plc

British Library Cataloguing in Publication Data
A CIP catalogue record for this book is available from the British Library

ISBN: 978-0-141-32413-5

For more fun and magic visit mrmagorium.co.uk

Now, of course, looking back, I know that we did have gifts. They were buried deep down inside our sunken, often wheezy chests. It turns out that even I had a gift or two, but back then no one knew it. Most of all, I didn't know it. But then something happened to me – a strange and odd and magical something – and it made me wonder. It made me think. It changed my life. And this is a short description of the something that happened:

The children at the Alton School for the Remarkably Giftless didn't go on many field trips. Our fine teacher, Mrs Tarblage, had explained that this was for our own good. We didn't go to zoos because too many of us were allergic to fur. We didn't go to aquariums because none of us could swim, and what if we fell into a tank? As a group we didn't have very good balance and so falling into a tank seemed likely. We didn't go to museums because we were the types of kids who often tripped, and it seemed like a bad idea to let us fall into a giant ancient statue that would tumble and crack into a million pieces.

But Mrs Tarblage did once take us on a surprise field trip right in the middle of an ordinary morning. She took us to the lobby of a bank – where Mrs Tarblage did her banking and needed to get into her safety deposit box. (This was during her unfortunate divorce from Mr Tarblage and was urgent as well as highly educational.) I should say that everyone at the Alton School for the Remarkably Giftless went to the bank but me. I got lost.

How did I get lost? Well, it was raining, for one thing – big thick sheets of rain. We weren't usually allowed out in the rain because so many of us were prone to colds and flus and sinus conditions. But this was an important educational opportunity, Mrs Tarblage said, and so we scuttled along bravely in a row of black umbrellas following the tall, lanky body of Mrs Tarblage and her sharp elbows through the city.

We were wearing name tags, too. Mine said:

Hello. My name is N. E. Bode. If lost, please return me to the Alton School for the Remarkably Giftless and gave the school address.

But, standing on a busy street corner in a clump of black umbrellas, a cab came round the bend, throwing a puddle of water all over me. I was soaking wet and cold and smelled like wet wool. I looked down at my name tag and it now read:

Hello – smear, smear – **N. E. Bode** – blur – **lost** – smear, blur –

Giftless – smear, smear, blur, blur . . .

I didn't want to be wearing such an awful name tag. It was one thing to be giftless, but lost and giftless was too much. And so I stopped to pick the name tag off. It left a smudgy, sticky rectangle on my anorak. I picked at that for a while, too. And then, when I looked up, I was still standing in a clump of black umbrellas. The crossing sign told us to walk and so we did. I walked with this clump of black umbrellas for twelve blocks until I found out that they were a Japanese tour group.

Did I mention that at some point during the Japanese tour the wind kicked my umbrella out of my hand and so I was completely drenched and unprotected?

When I realized that I was lost – and that I'd picked off the name tag with the school address on it – I ducked down an alley covered by a little overhang. I leaned up against the side of a building, breathless and terrified. How would I find my classmates and Mrs Tarblage? How would I find my way back to the school? Would I be lost forever?

I looked down the alley and saw an open cellar door. I thought it might be a place to sit down, dry off and think of a plan.

There were four steps leading into a basement. I walked down them.

It was dark – only one light glowing in a distant corner of the room, and there, splayed open in the dim light, was an enormous book, a book so enormous that the man standing over the book, scribbling in its pages, looked very small by comparison. But he wasn't small. The book was simply huge, gargantuan, like an overfed pig.

The man looked up from the book. He turned to me and looked at me over the top of his bifocals. He said, 'Bellini, here.' He stuck out his hand for me to shake it. I wiped my wet hand on my trousers and shook it.

'I'm N. E. Bode,' I said. 'Nice to meet you.'

'Are you lost?' he asked. 'You look lost.'

'I am lost,' I said. 'Mrs Tarblage was taking us on a field trip to the bank and then I got hit by a puddle and I had to take off my name tag and I got mixed up with some Japanese tourists and now I'm here.' I was the kind of kid who gives a lot of information all in one great gust of breath even if it didn't make much sense.

'Well, you seem a little nervous, a little flustered. Why don't you sit down and rest? I'll tell you a story or two so you can catch your breath and calm your nerves.'

'I'd like that,' I said. Mrs Tarblage didn't tell stories much, except about Mr Tarblage not taking out the rubbish when she'd clearly asked him to. All of her stories were the same: Mrs Tarblage the heroine, Mr Tarblage the villain. I wondered if Bellini knew Mr Tarblage, too, and if he'd tell a story about forgotten rubbish, but I didn't ask.

In fact, what happened was that Bellini never mentioned Mr or Mrs Tarblage. He picked up a slab of pages from the book and hefted them up and over, again and again, until he was near what would have to be the beginning of the book. 'Have you ever heard of Mr Edward Magorium?' he asked. 'And his amazing adventures?'

I shook my head no.

'Well, let's begin at the beginning, then.'

And so Bellini started reading.

Do I remember everything that was read to me that day? No, I don't. But I will always recall certain miraculous bits and hypnotizing pieces, and, most of all, how I felt while Bellini was reading me these stories. There was a tingling in my hands and whirring in my chest and breaking open of my imagination. I can't quite explain it beyond this. I was a soaking wet boy who smelled like wet wool who still had a sticky rectangle on his anorak where an embarrassing name tag used to be, a boy who'd always thought he was completely giftless, but I was also a boy tingling, whirring, breaking open.

What I've decided is that you should all know as much as I can recall just in case you want to know the amazing adventures of Edward Magorium too. And so

I've arranged all of the miraculous bits and hypnotizing pieces in this book: THE AMAZING COMPENDIUM OF EDWARD MAGORIUM – just for you, whoever you are, wherever you may be!

TABLE OF CONTENTS

GOLD, HUNTING IN ALASKA
GREAT CAPTURE THE FLAG GAME OF 1806
GRENCHEN, NATIONAL SWISS TOY FAIR

HAIGHT-ASHBURY
HIGH-FLYING AERONAUTICAL MAGORIUMS
HOLDERFIELD AND HIS BAND OF PIRATES
HOLMES, OLIVER WENDELL
HULA HOOP

INK, MAGICAL MAGORIUM
INNOVATOR OF COSMETIC DENTISTRY
ISLE OF WILD GOATS

JERNKLIN, SAD AND MOURNFUL
BUT BEAUTIFUL DEATH OF . . .

KALAMARIA – NATIONAL TOY FAIR OF GREECE
KELLER, HELEN
KING, BILLIE JEAN

LIVING THE HIGH LIFE
LIPLESS AMAZONIAN LIZARD EXPERT
LONDON, JACK

MAGORIUM BAND OF MANY SOUNDS
MAGORIUM SCHOOL OF QUESTIONS AND
CLOSE OBSERVATION
MAHJONG
MANCHU QING DYNASTY – GUANGXU, EMPEROR
MELVILLE, HERMAN
MOBY DICK
MONET, CLAUDE
MOON BOUNCE
MR MAGORIUM'S CREASED CONTRAPTION
OF GOSSAMER AVIATION

TABLE OF CONTENTS

Newton, Sir Isaac

Never-ending List of People Inspired by Edward Magorium

O'Keeffe, Georgia

Organ

Petites Curies

Polo

Q – the letter itself

Robinson, Jackie

Rubbery Blot
(a.k.a. Silly Putty)

Aerophone of the Lowest Bass Register
(a.k.a. the Tuba)

Edward Magorium was born Edward Magorium circa 1764. His earliest memory was the loud, low croaking sound of horns – nine of them to be exact – and the flapping of wings.

These were not just any horns. No, no. These were Aerophones of the Lowest Bass Register. We now have a simpler instrument and a simpler word for it: the *tuba*. But the tuba, as we know it, usually seen wrapped round some husky member of a marching band, didn't yet exist. The early version of the tuba was even more gargantuan than it is today. It was a serpentlike thing made of leather-encased wood and a mouthpiece fashioned from bone or ivory or oxhorn or pewter or some such. The monstrous instrument coiled and twisted and ballooned out at the end in an enormous funnel. It was a lot like breathing into a stiffened anaconda with holes where you could put your fingers to make notes, and it made the lowest, deepest sounds possible. Imagine the baritone singing voice of a two-hundred-kilogram frog.

For our purposes, instead of using the bulky phrase Aerophones of the Lowest Bass Register, I'll just stick to the word *tuba*. It's not correct, but it'll be easier.

Now one of the questions is: *why* was Edward Magorium's earliest memory the low croaking noises of tubas?

Well, it's simple really. His mother, Vlada Magorium, was a professional tuba player who held group tuba rehearsals for her nine-person tuba band on Monday, Wednesday and Friday afternoons for the tuba players of Lichtenstein with very high tuba aspirations. On Tuesdays and Thursdays, she held lessons for the children of Lichtenstein who wanted to become tuba players – all four of them. At the weekends, she practised alone.

Here are a few things you should know about Mrs Magorium. She had a whirlwind of hair on top of her head, and at night she always played soft tuba lullabies to put the children to sleep, and these lullabies always sounded like bedtime stories to Edward, filled with magic and twists and turns. Mrs Magorium was a practical woman overall, who liked the tidiness of marching musical notes and the predictable oompah of her instrument as well as predictability in her life. At first glance, you might think she was somewhat frail, but in fact she was extremely strong. In fact, she could have been a strong woman in a circus, but dedicated herself to the tuba instead.

The Magoriums' house was very small. Mr Magorium didn't make much money as a school teacher, and Mrs Magorium's nine-person tuba band had never been asked to hold a concert and so had never been paid. The tuba band was good – for a tuba band – but tuba bands, in general, are hard to listen to because all of the notes are so very, very low. Basically, the parlour echoed and rattled with the noise of nine very angry two-hundred-kilogram frogs. (Have I mentioned that the Magoriums spoke German? They spoke German because the people of Lichtenstein spoke German. It was the language of choice. And so if Mrs Magorium were describing her tuba music in terms of frogs – which she wouldn't, I don't think – she wouldn't have said the word *frog*. She'd have used the word *frosch*. Because I don't speak German, and never have, I'll just be using the English, which, I'm hoping, will suit you just fine. (If you want your books in German, go to the German language section!))

The tubas were so large that her nine-member band with all of their tubas barely fitted in the parlour. It didn't help that Vlada also repaired tubas and so the house was brimming with dented funnels, buckets of keys, chipped mouthpieces and busted tubing of various sorts. The three older Magorium children – Ansgar, Bernd and Brunhild – didn't fit in the house during rehearsals and so they sat quietly on the front steps – usually with their hands clamped over their ears.

And Edward was always with them – although he really loved tuba music. (One day, many, many years after Edward's childhood, he was painting model ships of the USS *Constitution* with his acquaintance Oliver Wendell Holmes who would tell him to take a music bath once or twice a week for a few seasons, because music is as good for the soul as bath water is for the body. And all his life, Edward always tried to get into the tub, every so often, and fill it with music and take a long soak.)

The Magoriums didn't have enough money for a

cradle or pram and so Edward's father made them himself. He was the kind of man who could make almost anything when he needed to, but he never thought that anything he made was very special. His cradles and prams were made out of tuba parts – funnels and tubing. Ansgar, Bernd and Brunhild wrapped Edward snugly in a blanket, placed him in the handmade tuba pram and often pushed him to the Aviary across the street. An Aviary (see Aviary below) is a home for birds.

Children were not allowed in the Aviary. And so Ansgar, Bernd and Brunhild would cup their hands to the window and look inside. Bernd and Brunhild always shoved each other because each of them thought that the other was trying to get a better spot at the glass. (Bernd and Brunhild loved to argue with each other.) And Ansgar would stand there silently. He was the silent type. No one ever asked any questions about the birds – why they were certain colours, why they sang different songs, why they swooped when they swooped. First of all, none of them thought they knew the answers and second of all, the Magorium children had learned not to ask questions. (See Asking Questions below.)

Edward was so young that his eyesight was still

a little blurry. But, from his snuggly spot in the tuba-funnel pram, he knew he loved the birds. (He wouldn't have used the word *bird*, though. He'd have used the German word *vogel*.)

And, as he grew old enough to waddle up to the Aviary's glass and cup his own hands and stare inside, he decided that he might become a bird one day, if given the chance.

AGE OF ENLIGHTENMENT

All of this – the tuba-playing, the bird-watching, the pram-pushing Magorium children – took place during the 1700s, known as the Age of Enlightenment, but regular people living regular lives didn't go around feeling enlightened all of the time. What I mean is that it may have been the Age of Enlightenment when it came to things like philosophy and logic and economics, but there were still plagues, wars, itchy woollen clothing and very little fresh fruit – and, on top of all of that, people rarely bathed. The 1700s didn't smell very good. Mr and Mrs Magorium had slowly stopped being observers of the world and askers-of-questions, because life was difficult. They were simply trying to survive. And that is why Ansgar, Bernd and Brunhild also didn't ask any questions with their cupped faces pressed to the Aviary window.

Questions are like that. One person stops asking them and then another and another until finally they all dry up and disappear.

ASKING QUESTIONS

Eventually, Edward Magorium would change all of this non-question-asking.

He was not an early talker. His mind was too busy to make words. He was smelling the world – woolly and smoky. He was tasting the world – beefy and potato stewy. He was touching the world – horse-hair sofa-y and warm waxy. He was listening to the world – loud, low croaky and bird twittery. He was watching the world – rainy, sunny, dusty, gusty, glinty, shiny, dusky.

But one day when he was five years old, he was at the Aviary window with Ansgar, Bernd, Brunhild – and the three newer Magoriums: Walburga, Rambert and Ulrika – the last of which was being pushed in a handmade tuba-funnel pram. (Edward was smack in the middle of seven children.) His mother's tuba band rehearsal had just finished and the street was suddenly pretty quiet.

Edward tugged on Ansgar's shirt sleeve and said his very first sentence, 'Excuse me, I have a question.'

'A question . . .' Ansgar said, as if he'd heard the word a long time ago but couldn't quite remember what it meant.

'He has a question,' Brunhild said.

'No, he doesn't,' Bernd argued. 'No one just suddenly has a question.'

'Yes, he does!' Brunhild shouted.

'No, he doesn't!' Bernd shouted back.

'I think I do,' Edward said.

The three newest Magoriums just stared up at him all wide-eyed.

Edward said, 'My question is: why?'

'Why . . .' Ansgar said, as if he'd heard the word a long time ago but couldn't quite remember what it meant.

'That's not a real question!' Brunhild shouted.

'Yes, it is!' Bernd shouted back.

And then one of the little Magoriums, Rambert, who had just learned how to waddle up to the Aviary window and cup his hands to the glass, asked his own question, 'Why what?'

Everyone stopped and stared at Rambert.

'Why, why, why?' asked little Walburga.

'Wh, wh, wh?' asked the littlest Magorium, Ulrika, sitting up in her tuba funnel.

And that is the way it is with questions. Once someone asks one, they swell and pop up everywhere.

AVIARY

And it was at the Aviary window – watching the flight patterns of birds – standing alongside a few cats (who also liked to watch the flight patterns of birds – but with different, darker intentions), that Edward Magorium felt a tingling in his hands and whirring in his chest and breaking open of his imagination. It's much like the way I felt while Bellini was reading the Big Book to me, and I've come to realize that it's the way many people feel when you feel something deep down that is important to you, that is changing you. I can't quite explain it beyond this. He was just a regular boy holding his cupped hands up to a window, the son of a school teacher and a tuba player, a boy who was tingling, whirring, breaking open.

BIRD FEATHERS

I should also mention that shortly after that moment at the Aviary window, Edward stole his way into the Aviary. Bellini went into great detail here – how Edward found an open grate and brought flowers and gave them to the Aviary-keeper so that he wouldn't just throw him out on his ear immediately. These details have become a little blurry, but this fact remains: Edward volunteered to sweep up the Aviary. He told the Aviary-keeper, an angry birdlike man with teeth as sharp as a beak, that he'd sweep up every day in exchange for the feathers he'd collected.

The Aviary-keeper loved birds, but hated feathers. They were everywhere! He found them at night in his hair, in his shoes, in his pockets. He agreed.

And so, without telling anyone, Edward swept up the feathers every day and put them in a sack.

He didn't tell anyone because he wanted to surprise them. Actually, he wanted his mother and father to step out of the house one day and call his name while all of his brothers and sisters were there so that he could appear in the sky overhead and flap down to them, as if nothing were unusual in the least. He was determined to fly. One day, he was going to make a pair of wings! *Wings!* (Or, well, as Edward would have said it back then, if he were going to say it, which he wasn't because it was secret – *flugel!*)

BIRTHDAYS

Birthdays during the 1700s were bleak and dismal by our standards. There were no backyard bouncy castles, bowling parties or trick birthday candles that force kids to accidentally spit all over birthday cakes. And, of course, people back then were still itchy because of their woolly clothes, ate very little fresh fruit and didn't smell very good.

The bouncy castle wouldn't be invented until 1957 (see Scurlock under the Ss for the full story). Bowling had been around forever but not in alleys with bumper guards and rentable shoes. And trick candles started out as wind-resistant candles and wouldn't show up for another hundred years – and even then it would take time before some evil genius thought to put them on a cake to torture children.

(I have to say that my own birthdays were bleak and dismal. My parents didn't have any money for big celebrations, and the children at the Alton School for the Remarkably Giftless couldn't eat much cake – we were allergic to flour, sugar, chocolate and gelatins – and, of course, there'd once been an unfortunate incident where someone had sent their fringe up in smoke while trying to blow out candles. And I'm not even going to go into the complete panic and confusion caused by the blindfolded spinning that's part of Pin the Tail on the Donkey.)

But in the 1700s people didn't even always jot your birthday down when you were born, and, because those infants were too young and not-yet-fully-functioning, they couldn't very well jot their birthdays down themselves. If someone had taken the time to write down the day you were born then you had a better chance that someone might remember your birthday. Your mother or father might give you a little something – like a sugar-crusted prune, but that was about it. If they gave you a toy, it would likely be something like marbles or chalk or maybe some pick-up sticks. The strange thing is that you would have been very happy about a sugar-crusted prune back in those days – not to mention marbles, chalk or sticks – mainly because you didn't know that bouncy castles and bowling parties and trick birthday candles would one day exist.

Lucky for Edward Magorium, his parents had written down his birthday and remembered it. On his tenth birthday, they still lived in the little house stuffed with tuba parts across the street from the Aviary. They'd just eaten soup out of bowl-shaped tuba parts with spoons made out of tuba keys. And Edward's mother gave a sugar-crusted prune to each of the Magorium children for dessert. (She'd recently been paid to be in a tuba concert and this was a real splurge.) All of the children gazed at their sugar-crusted prunes.

'Go ahead!' Mrs Magorium said. 'Enjoy!'

Some of the children nibbled at them. Ansgar took one small bite, wrapped his up in a napkin and saved the next bite for later. But Edward opened his mouth wide and popped his sugar-crusted prune into his mouth whole. He wanted the full effect. It tasted sugary and pruney, and he was very happy.

But that wasn't the end of this birthday. No, no. His father handed him a very small rectangular gift. 'Open it!' his father said.

Edward unfolded the packaging and opened up a little box to find an even littler book inside. The book was tiny, minuscule. It was so very small that it made Edward's small hands look like those of a giant. He picked up the book, thumbed through its pages. They were blank. He wasn't sure what to do exactly. He didn't want to tell his father that he'd been tricked into buying a book with no words in it. But then his father said, 'It's for you to fill. You have a lot of little ideas. I could only afford the smallest book, but I thought you might want to jot some of your ideas down.'

Edward did have a lot of ideas. In fact, it seemed like his head was swarming with ideas, notions, configurations, puzzles, dreams. Many of them had to do with the Aviary across the street. Birds flapping, flying, whirring and darting – and his plan to make a pair of wings. How did the birds fly, exactly? How did they do it? Edward had a few ideas.

That very evening, in fact, he went to the bedroom he shared with his six brothers and sisters, and he drew wings – not any old wings. He drew wings strapped to the back of a boy – a boy that looked a lot like Edward Magorium. He added details until his eyes got blurry with sleep and then he shut the book and wrote on its cover:

BOOK OF LITTLE IDEAS by EDWARD MAGORIUM.

BOOK OF LITTLE IDEAS

Edward Magorium took his Book of Little Ideas with him wherever he went. He jotted notes on wings, of course, but also the way leaves drifted down from trees, the way puddles reflected his face in distorted ripples, the way his youngest sister collected food in her hair – was she saving it for later?

As a result, The Book of Little Ideas grew. At first it fitted loosely in his trouser pocket, but then it got fatter and longer and wider. Soon it couldn't fit in his pocket any more. He had to slip it in with his school books. And then it was too big to carry to school and he had to keep it under his bed.

He became a believer in . . .

CLOSE OBSERVATION

I f you tell a child to draw a picture of a flower, they usually very quickly draw a circle surrounded by looping deformed-looking bunny ears. When, in fact, Edward Magorium could have told you, even at a young age, that most flowers don't look anything like a circle of strange bunny ears. (One day, years after Edward had grown up, he would be taking a walk with his good friend, the artist Georgia O'Keeffe, in New Mexico, collecting odd bits and pieces of bones and desert flowers as they went. She put it kind of like this: Nobody sees a flower – really – it's so small it takes time. We don't have time and to see takes time, like having a friend takes time. And Edward never forgot it.)

Next time you see a flower, use close observation.

You'll notice yawning mouths, droopy heads, maybe a few beady eyes and pursed lips. The petals might be velvety. The stems might be furry or barbed. A flower might smell flowery, but it also might smell stale or sour. If you listen to a flower, you might be surprised by what it has to say to you.

Edward Magorium always was. He jotted all flowers and flower conversations in his Book of Little Ideas.

In school, he found out that he wasn't the first person to believe in questions and close observations. He wasn't the first person to have a book of little ideas. He stumbled upon the work of:

COPERNICUS

Copernicus was a Pole – and I don't mean he was pole-shaped like something you'd find in a basement holding up the ceiling. I mean Polish – though I should mention that the Germans decided a long time ago that he was German. He had very dark eyebrows and lived in places called things like: Royal Prussia (which sounds like the name of a very furry hat) and Warmia (which isn't actually very warm) and Frawenburg (which sounds like something I made up, but I didn't). He studied in places like Bologna (not to be confused with baloney, the round meat that comes in plastic containers and is delicious when fried) and Ferrara (not to be confused with the very fast car). He jotted notes about the universe. He was the one who figured out that the Earth revolves round the Sun – and not the other way round.

Edward became obsessed with Copernicus, and when Edward became obsessed with things, his brothers and sisters were more than a little afraid of him, because he always had some kind of idea of his own.

When it came to Copernicus, Edward decided to make a living solar system. He wanted it to float in space like the real solar system.

He decided to talk his brothers and sisters – the older ones: Ansgar, Bernd, Brunhild, and the younger ones: Walburga, Rambert and Ulrika – into being planets, the sun and the moon. Ansgar was the hardest to convince. Ever since Edward started asking questions, Ansgar hadn't been able to stop. (One day, many years from this day, Edward would be reminded of this day. He would be practising a violin duet with his good friend – though not very good violinist – Albert Einstein when Albert, quite out of the blue, put down his violin and told him that the important thing was not to stop questioning. 'Curiosity,' he said, 'has its own reason for existing.' And then he picked his violin back up and counted, 'And a-one and a-two and a-three!')

'Why do we have to do this?' Ansgar asked Edward. 'Are you sure everything revolves round the Sun? Do you think these ropes will hold us up? Are those tree limbs strong enough? What kind of tree is this? Does it bloom in the summer?' And on and on and on . . .

He insisted on being the Sun as he was the oldest.

Bernd and Brunhild were difficult too. They fought over which one got to be the Earth, because they always fought.

Edward found an enormous sprawling tree in a distant field. He dressed them all in costumes – yellow for the Sun, a ring round Saturn, etc. etc. – and suspended them from various limbs with ropes where they bobbed and swayed. The children hated it until people began to show up, of course, to see why children were suspended from tree limbs. Even Bernd and Brunhild stopped fighting when the crowd was there. Edward gave lessons to the good people of Lichtenstein on the universe while Ansgar asked questions from his spot in the tree. 'When was Copernicus born? Why is that woman wearing that hat? Is that a beetle? What kind of beetle is that?'

Edward forged on.

And, maybe even more than Copernicus, he admired . . .

DA VINCI – AS IN LEONARDO DA VINCI

D a Vinci was a famous artist – the one who
painted the Mona Lisa (that woman who's
kind of smirking and is now used in advertisements
for things like ketchup). But da Vinci also thought
up things like: the submarine, a diving suit made out
of pig skin and a hose connected to air, the calcula-
tor and solar energy. He was also very interested in
flight, like Edward. He designed a helicopter – except
that it also spun the people inside – the hang-glider
and a parachute.

And he was a constant jotter of notes in books of
ideas. He often wrote his notes backwards – a secret
language – siht ekil gnihtemos tnew taht.

After Edward started learning about da Vinci,
he started making inventions of his own. He took

notes on the birds in the Aviary, as always, when he was there sweeping up feathers after hours. He loved the feel of the birds flapping and twittering around his head. He scratched away in his Book of Little Ideas – which was growing fatter. He talked Bernd and Brunhild, who were now used to heights and ropes when suspended in the tree, into testing his own versions of the parachute and hang-glider – which were wobbly and flimsy and not very effective.

Edward studied da Vinci's notes on diving costumes and submarines, and scratched away in his Book of Little Ideas – which was growing even fatter. He talked Rambert and Walburga into testing his underwater diving suit in a nearby lake. It sometimes worked and sometimes didn't. Rambert and Walburga got very good at holding their breath and swimming quickly to the surface.

Edward studied da Vinci's notes on solar energy, and scratched away in his Book of Little Ideas – which was growing fatter than ever. And he tried to talk Ansgar into holding mirrors near the lake on sunny days to capture the sun's energy, but he couldn't convince him. By this point, Ansgar had become tired of people not knowing all of the

The boys – Ansgar, Bernd, Rambert and Edward – all got boy dolls. The girls – Brunhild, Walburga and Ulrika – all got girl dolls.

Furthermore, Ansgar, whose brow was always furrowed with a look of deep concentration, had a doll whose brow was always furrowed with a look of deep concentration.

Bernd and Brunhild, who shouted loudly at each other when not suspended from a tree or working together when about to jump from some high place with a handmade parachute or hang-glider attached to their backs, had dolls that looked like they were shouting loudly.

Rambert and Walburga, who were often practising holding their breath even when they weren't underwater testing Edward's diving costumes, had dolls with inflated cheeks as if holding their breath.

Ulrika's doll smiled a crooked-toothed smile.

And Edward's doll wore a perplexed expression as if observing something very closely and about to ask a question.

Edward would stare at his doll, observing it closely, and finally asked the doll a question. 'Were you made to look like me?' he asked.

The doll didn't answer.

'Were you made to look like me?' he asked again, a little louder and angrier.

The doll didn't answer.

Edward's cheeks flushed with frustration.

The doll's face went red too.

Edward looked away from the doll and then back again. He had an idea. He pretended to start to cry.

And the doll's eyes turned teary and wet.

'Aha!' he shouted, and he waved his arms in the air, victoriously. He smiled – a big, huge happy smile.

And the doll smiled too!

This was an amazing doll! A doll that matched the ever-changing expressions of its owner! Who had invented such a thing? Who was the amazing mind behind this doll? Edward had to know!

The doll had come in a box with one word written on it: Jernklin. Who was this Jernklin and how could Edward meet him?

Much to his dismay, he remembered then that the dolls had come all the way from Luxembourg. Edward was only twelve years old. When would he ever get from Lichtenstein to Luxembourg?

He sat on the floor – slumping glumly.

The doll slumped glumly too.

DROUGHT – AS IN THE GREAT TUBA DROUGHT
OF THE 18TH CENTURY

The first sign that something was going horribly, horribly wrong with the tubas of Lichtenstein was the sour smell. Each time one of the players bellowed out a low note (and all tuba notes are low notes), foul fumes rose up from the funnels in a gust. Even when just lying still in a corner, the fumes began to seep from the keys. The Magorium house began to smell like socks that needed to be boiled – remember that the Age of Enlightenment was woolly and stinky and things like socks often needed to be boiled.

Mrs Magorium didn't let this stop her from practising, however. The Lichtenstein Band of Many Sounds had a lot of concerts now. She had to keep at it, and she did. She lifted the windows to air out the house. As soon as she picked up her tuba, all of the Magorium kids darted off in various directions – some with books of little ideas, others with bundled parachutes, others with diving gear and the littlest with a mirror. They all wanted to get away from the stench.

But then on one terrible day, the tuba's throat choked up. The note sounded like something being gargled and then spat out. Mrs Magorium picked up a spare tuba. It had the same problem.

She then went to the house of one of her fellow tuba players and found the man weeping over his sour, choked instrument.

It was the same with tubas all over Lichtenstein. Not only were they sour and choked, they were also turning brittle and drying up like corn husks.

This went on for months. All of the tubas perished. There was nothing to do but move on. There was a rumour that tubas were still healthy in Luxembourg.

The Magoriums loaded up their things and got on a train.

And there was Edward Magorium, staring out of the train window at night. All of the other Magorium children were fast asleep; even Ansgar had nodded off while making notes on a toad he had brought with him for close observation in a small box. (He wasn't actually writing ON the toad, of course. He had his own Book of Little Ideas to jot in.) Edward was leaning against his collection of feathers in the feather sack that he called a pillow so that no one would be suspicious. He also had his Jernklin doll with him. He was too old for dolls, but the Jernklin doll wasn't just any doll. Edward and his Jernklin doll stared out of the window together – two sets of eyes – one pair glass, one real – darting over the landscape and up at the night sky. The sky was filled with stars and they shone like candles.

Edward was going to Luxembourg! And he was thinking only one thing: find Jernklin.

EDISON, THOMAS

And this is where I should put Thomas Edison. Right here in the Es. And here he comes, marching this way. I can see his large head with its broad brow. He's muttering to himself about electricity and what not.

It's true that one day when Edward Magorium is a grown man, he will spend rainy afternoons locked in noughts-and-crosses battles with Edison. So true! This is where Edward Magorium is headed. This is the direction his long, long life will take . . .

But should I get into Edison now? Right in the middle of the search for Jernklin – the extraordinary toymaker who will change Edward's young life forever?

Edison's head snaps up which surprises me.

I hadn't known that I was talking out loud – and probably pretty loudly, too, since Edison was nearly deaf.

'It's a compendium!' he reminds me. 'It's in alphabetical order! Not first come, first served!'

'I know,' I tell him. 'But could you do me a favour and go on back? Just for now? I'll get to you later. I promise!'

And now back to the search for Jernklin . . . (If desperate for Edison, please go to page 85.)

EMPORIUM OF JERNKLIN'S WONDER DOLLS

Life in Luxembourg, like life in Lichtenstein, was itchy; there was little fresh fruit and people didn't smell very good. But Edward didn't mind. He preferred Luxembourg, which was bigger and more bustling. There were more things to look at and all of the things were new. So all of them deserved close observation with fresh eyes and a new set of questions altogether.

While Mr Magorium set up the *Luxembourg* Magorium School of Questions and Close Observation and Mrs Magorium delighted in playing healthy tubas again, setting up a new band – now called the *Luxembourg* Band of Many Sounds,

Edward walked the city streets, looking in stores for ever-changing dolls.

He asked shopkeeper after shopkeeper. None of them had ever heard of such a thing, and they often thought he was not-right-in-the-head.

'An ever-changing doll? Don't be ridiculous!'

'Don't waste my time with such nonsense, you addle-brained boy!'

And, more to the point, 'Get out of here!'

More than once Edward was chased by shopkeepers angrily shaking brooms at him. (The shopkeepers of Luxembourg in the 1700s were fond of shaking brooms at children. In fact, maybe they still are. I've never been to Luxembourg myself.)

Edward also asked children. Luckily they weren't armed with brooms, but they didn't believe him any more than the shopkeepers.

He decided that he had to stop trying to find Jernklin to give Jernklin a chance to find him. His Jernklin doll had found him, after all, and so Jernklin would have to, too.

And this is what happened more or less.

Edward decided it was time to make his wings. He had enough feathers and some lightweight cotton from his father's old shirts. At night he glued feathers to the cotton, which he billowed from straps attached to each of his arms and harnessed round his back in a bow. The wings looked like they would work, but looking like they would work didn't mean anything really, if they didn't work. Before he could swoop down and surprise his family, he first needed to test his wings.

And so very early one Saturday morning, he snuck out of the house with his wings in a sack and walked to an open grassy area in Luxembourg. The shopkeepers with their angry brooms hadn't yet opened their doors. The only audience Edward had was a few birds sitting on a statue. They watched him put the wings on and strap the harness and tighten the bow. He flapped the wings a few times in place – a quick practice. And then he took off running. He ran as hard and as fast as he possibly could, and then he started to flap. He flapped as hard and fast as he possibly could. And at just that moment there was a small gust of wind. Edward could feel his wings catch the breeze and pop open – taut at his back. One of his shoes hit a clump of dirt and he stumbled, but he didn't fall. No, no, he was buoyed by the wind, just enough to lift him off the ground for a second, the smallest tiniest second. His feet kept running, but for this smallest tiniest second they were only churning through air.

Then the wind stopped, as wind can. His wings went slack. He fell to the ground – hard this time. The birds cawed and flapped their own wings – showing off – and flew away.

That would have been that. The end. But, sitting just to the side of the statue, watching the entire thing as well, was a very hungry, very quick cat. He smelled the glue that Edward had used, yes, but he smelled the wings too. Real wings. This must be a real bird, he thought. A real and really big bird.

The cat caught Edward in his steely gaze. Edward stared back.

'Hello, Kitty,' he said, not knowing that this would one day be an entire Japanese toy industry of its own.

The cat crouched and then pounced and ran after Edward. Edward took off. He flapped his wings, but they were useless. In fact now, without the wind, they weighed him down. He ran out of the park and down one street, then another. The cat kept on coming, its long lean body fast on his heels.

He darted down one alleyway and then another

and another until finally the cat had given up and was nowhere to be seen.

But now Edward was in a part of the city that he'd never seen before. There were all of these tiny little speciality shops. Instead of a butcher, there was a shop that only sold pig's knuckles. Instead of a flower store, there was a shop that only sold orange bristle-headed mums. Instead of a clothing store, there was a shop that only sold gloves – not pairs, but one by one, for people who'd lost just one of a pair. Breathless and feathery and a little dizzy, Edward stared up and down the street. He didn't know where he was. His wings hadn't worked and now they looked shabby, patchy and ruined – and he was lost! He looked up at the sun to figure out north, south, east and west. But grew dizzier and fell to the kerb on his rump. He felt like he was going to cry. One day, many, many years later, Edward would be reminded of this day. He would have just lost a game of polo to Winston Churchill. And Churchill, a good sport, really, would lean from his horse towards Edward and tell him that success is really just the ability to go from one failure to another with no loss of enthusiasm. Although Edward hadn't heard these wise words just yet, he already knew he couldn't give in to failure. He had to buck up.

And that is when he felt the large warm hand on his shoulder.

'Are you unwell?' a voice above him said.

He turned and looked up. There was an elderly man with white whiskers and a pomp of white hair sitting like foamy whipped cream on his head. And behind his head was a store. It wasn't a toy store. It was a shop that only sold one type of toy – dolls – and only one kind of doll, in fact. A Wonder Doll.

The store was called: The Emporium of Jernklin's Wonder Dolls!

Edward hadn't found Jernklin. Jernklin had found him! At last!

(And the wings – those *flugels*! – had worked in a strange way, too, hadn't they? Flapping him right to the spot he wanted to be!)

EXPERT

Jernklin was an expert. And Edward spent years in his dusty workshop among all of the doll parts – little wooden hands and feet, glass eyes, paint sets – trying to learn how to make Jernklin's Wonder Dolls. He learned about wiring their wooden joints and pasting on their wigs and fitting on their tiny shoes.

Meanwhile, he also kept up with his own Book, which was growing bigger and fatter still, and no longer fitted in any drawers. And he went to school. He admired a certain American named Benjamin Franklin – a brilliant scientist, politician, writer and the most famous kite-flyer of all time – and Newton who thought up gravity because he was the kind of person to ask the question: why does an apple fall *down* out of a tree and not up or sideways? He once scratched his name into a library window sill at The King's School in Grantham where it can still be seen today. Although no one preserved any acts of vandalism from Edward Magorium, he graduated from the Magorium School of Questions and Close Observation at age twelve and then attended the Luxembourg National University, where he completed all of his studies in a record five days! (One day, many years from his graduation, Edward would tell this story to his friend Mark Twain while scrapbooking – one of Twain's favourite hobbies – both of them using one of Mark Twain's Patent Scrapbooks. Twain turned to him and said, 'Well, Magorium, I like how you didn't let school get in the way of your education!')

Edward was an academic success, but he knew that he really wanted to be a toymaking success. Jernklin took him under his wing and taught him everything he knew. There was a problem, however, in his apprenticeship with Jernklin. When it came to making the Jernklin doll faces, things always went wrong. Their faces always came out with looks of frustration and despair and longing, which were the emotions that Edward always felt when trying to make them work.

Jernklin would tell Edward that he was putting himself into the dolls. 'You have to remove yourself,' he told Edward, 'and think only of the child who will delight in the doll. This process isn't about the maker. It's about the gift.'

Jernklin was patient. He would watch and nod and sometimes run a ruffling hand through his foamy wisp of white hair. (Years later, Edward would remember Jernklin's patience as a teacher. He would be playing a game of mah-jong with the Chinese Emperor Guangxu, fiddling with his tiles and talking about how he felt like he'd failed Jernklin. Guangxu would tell him the old Chinese proverb, 'Teachers open the door. You enter by yourself.' Edward thought maybe he could open doors for others one day. Maybe.)

Because Edward loved old Jernklin so much and wanted to impress him, he would try harder and harder. After years in the workshop – Edward growing taller but not too tall, and wider but not too wide – he never made a single Wonder Doll that didn't look like his own face, flexed in frustration.

FINDING YOUR WAY IN THE WORLD

O ne day, Edward was working behind the counter of Jernklin's shop. The shop was empty. It was usually empty. Jernklin didn't like to advertise. The walls were lined with dolls, all staring out of the window, waiting for children to come and claim them.

Jernklin walked out of the workshop in the back of the store and made a proclamation. 'It's time for you to find your way in the world, Edward.'

'What?' Edward said. He'd decided that this was his way in the world. He was going to learn to make Jernklin dolls. He had to! He couldn't quit! 'But I'm staying here to learn to be an expert. I can't quit now!'

'Why not?' Jernklin said. 'You have to make room to become your own expert.'

'My own expert?' Edward said. 'In what?'

'I don't know,' Jernklin said. 'But if you find your way in the world, the path will lead you to it.' Jernklin loved Edward. His eyes filled with tears. There was one doll that was not for sale in the shop. It was the original Jernklin doll that Jernklin had made when he was just a boy. Now it was old and had a foamy wisp of white hair on its head. The doll's eyes teared up too. 'Go on,' Jernklin said. He grabbed Edward by the shoulders and gave him a sturdy hug and then he let him go. 'Go and find your way in the world.'

FRENCH EMPEROR-TO-BE – NAPOLEON

Before Edward set out to find his way in the world, he asked Jernklin if he could take a trunk of Wonder Dolls with him so that he could sell them for Jernklin, who never had much money, and to help spread the word. Jernklin agreed. And so Edward and his Book of Ideas and his trunk of Jernklin dolls set out in hopes of finding a way in the world.

For years Edward travelled and sold the dolls. He saw Vienna (where he suggested to a wonderful butcher that he roll his sausages much smaller and tighter) and Pisa (where he suggested to an architect that he not redo the design of a certain tower so that it wouldn't be like every other tower) and London (where he lost his pocket watch and suggested to everyone he met that the city needed an enormous clock that kept good time so that everyone could go watch-less).

Edward landed in Paris in 1795 and, on the outskirts of the city, he set up a little stand of Jernklin dolls. It was early November and chilly and the Jernklin dolls were shivering in their boxes, and Edward was shivering in his thin coat. Paris had a new celebrity – a short corporal with shiny black hair who liked to keep one hand stuffed in his waistcoat between the shiny buttons. His name was Napoleon Bonaparte. One day when Edward was at his stand of dolls, shivering away, Napoleon himself clomped by on an enormous horse. He was waving to some of the common folk when the Jernklin dolls caught his eye – one Jernklin doll in particular, who had shiny black hair and a hand stuffed in his waistcoat between his shiny buttons.

Napoleon stopped, dismounted and examined the doll.

'Would you like to buy it?' Edward asked.

Napoleon blushed and put the doll down quickly. 'Of course not! I'm a great military leader! I don't buy *dolls*!' (I should note that Napoleon was speaking French because he was French. So he didn't say *dolls*. He said *poupées*, which is funny to us because it sounds a lot like the word *poopies*, but isn't funny to them because their word for *poopies* doesn't sound like *poupées*.) Then Napoleon's eyes flashed. 'However,' he said, raising his pointy chin, 'I would like a toymaker to create stiff little toy *soldiers*, *not dolls*, so that I can give them as gifts to my brave men.'

'Yes, sir,' Edward said. He was cold and hungry and trying to find his way in the world. (Also, people didn't usually say no to Napoleon. He wasn't the type to be pushed around.)

And so Edward had his first real commissioned work as a toymaker. He began by researching toy soldiers, looking at everything on the market. The toy soldiers were always rigid. They had blank eyes and blank faces. They stood at attention, row after row of them. Then Edward set out to see real soldiers – Napoleon's men practising for battle. They were not rigid or blank. They lunged and dove and dodged and staggered and leapt and strode and hunched and crawled and sprung. Their eyes would grow wide with fear and then slitted with focus, darting and glaring and staring. Their faces were serious and shocked and brooding and worried and confused and brave.

Edward remembered Jernklin's old advice. 'You have to remove yourself,' he'd told Edward, 'and think only of the child who will delight in the doll. This process isn't about the maker. It's about the gift.' He imagined Jernklin's patient nod, his old liver-spotted hand ruffling through his foamy wisp of white hair.

Edward removed himself. He thought of the soldiers who didn't want little rigid, blank versions of themselves. They wanted the truth. This wasn't about Edward. It was about the gift.

And so Edward fashioned dolls from clay, dolls that lunged, dove, dodged, staggered, leapt, strode, hunched, crawled and sprung with eyes wide with fear and slitted with focus, that darted, glared, stared out of faces that were serious, shocked, brooding, worried, confused and brave.

He spent one afternoon in Napoleon's parlour while he was out, arranging the toy soldiers the way he'd seen the real soldiers practising for battle in an elaborate scene on the floor. Then he covered them with a thin sheet and waited for Napoleon to come home. He also brought with him Jernklin's doll that looked so much like Napoleon. He sat it in an armchair.

When Napoleon arrived, he was tired, grumbling about trouble in Italy. He saw Edward and said, 'Oh, you. Not today! Not today!'

'That's fine, sir,' Edward said, and, with that, he lifted the white sheet and started to fold it.

That's when Napoleon saw the toy soldiers. He froze. 'What is this?'

'The gifts for your soldiers,' Edward said. 'I'll bring them another day.'

'No!' Napoleon shouted. He was a shouter by nature. 'They're amazing! They're brilliant! I love them!'

'You do?'

'Of course!' Napoleon said. 'They're perfect!'

He shouted to an assistant who'd been standing guard by the door. 'Get me a map of Italy – as big as they come! We'll use these soldiers – so real, so true to life – to plan our strategy!' Napoleon was beaming, as was the Jernklin doll of Napoleon.

Edward balled the sheet up in his hands. 'They're toys,' he said. 'Gifts.'

'Not any more!' Napoleon told him. 'They're perfect for military strategy! Why hadn't I thought of it before? We'll plan our attack tonight!'

'They're toys,' Edward said. 'They aren't supposed

to be used to plan attacks! You – you, can't!' Edward said.

The room went quiet. 'What did you say to me?' Napoleon asked, his black hair shining, his hand stuffed in his waistcoat between the shiny buttons.

'You can't!' Edward said, and, with that, he stamped on the toy soldiers which, made of clay, broke into tiny bits under his shoes.

'OUT!' Napoleon shouted. 'OUT WITH YOU! GET OUT! LEAVE FRANCE! DON'T COME BACK!'

Two guards lifted Edward by each arm, yanked him off the ground to the door and threw him out on the street.

Edward stood up, brushed himself off and walked home with his own chin held high, but he often wondered what became of Jernklin's doll of Napoleon. Did Napoleon have it destroyed because he was too embarrassed by it? Did he hide it under his bed? Did he sleep with it at night when he was the ruler of France? Did he take it with him to Waterloo and on his unsuccessful attempt to escape to the good old US of A (which wasn't very old back then)? Was he clutching the Jernklin doll when he died on that island called Saint Helena and breathed his final words, *'Tête d'Armée!'* which means Head of Army, which he was through and through to the end.

FUTURES FOR EDWARD'S BROTHERS AND SISTERS

Who knows what Edward's brothers and sisters would have become if he hadn't started asking questions that then wouldn't stop, if he hadn't suspended them from trees and had them testing parachutes and hang-gliders and diving costumes and asked them to spend long periods of time holding mirrors?

By the time Edward had packed his bag – with his Jernklin doll inside it – and had hugged his parents goodbye and was heading out to find his way in the world, his brothers and sisters already knew their ways in the world, and were beginning their adventures.

Ansgar went off with his own Book of Ideas in search of more questions and more answers. He wound up in Argentina and became fascinated with their Lipless Lizard. In fact, he lived among the Lipless Amazonian Lizards, learning their ways, speaking their tongue-flicking language, eating a lot of Amazonian ants. He became a renowned and beloved scientist who wrote much on the subject of close scientific observation.

Bernd and Brunhild became the High-Flying Aeronautical Magoriums who travelled the world, amazing crowds with their high-wire wrestling matches. They had become fearless when it came to heights, and still had a desire to fight each other. They put the two talents together and *voila*! They were a team!

Rambert and Walburga often joined them. They travelled with a see-through tank and did acrobatics underwater all the while holding their breath for extremely long periods of time. They became the famous Amphibious Frog Magoriums.

Ulrika also found her calling in life very early. Fascinated by her own crooked teeth, she set out to invent contraptions for training teeth and for replacing lost teeth. She became very famous as a cosmetic dentistry innovator, and had a gorgeous smile.

And Edward? Well, he didn't yet know that he was THE Edward Magorium. He didn't know what he was going to be or do. And he'd already failed at making Jernklin dolls because he wasn't Jernklin. But who was he? And what would *he* make?

Great Capture the Flag Game of 1806

Sorely disappointed with all things short and shouty and hand-stuffy-in-waistcoaty, Edward again set out to find his way in the world. He ended up in Germany at the Brothers Grimm house one day. It was a little hot, and there was the slack air of long summer afternoons with nothing to do.

Jacob wanted to talk about languages, how one sound slips into another over the years, and jot notes.

Wilhelm disagreed. 'We always do that! We should entertain our fine guest, Mr Magorium.' He turned to Edward. 'What would you like to do?'

Edward was looking out of the window to a stand of trees. It would be cooler in a forest, he thought. 'Let's play a little game,' he said. 'Just a bit of Capture the Flag in the woods out of the glare of the sun.' He didn't say Capture the Flag, of course, because he was in Germany speaking German to Germans.

Wilhelm nodded, 'Yes, let's!'

Jacob sighed and agreed.

And they were off.

The game started quietly. Jacob and Wilhelm versus Edward. But it was a heated competition. Night came and the game didn't end. A week passed, and still there was no winner.

Soon, word of the game spread, and children started to show up, choosing sides and joining in. Every day more children arrived from the surrounding towns and farmlands. Eventually there were hundreds of children playing throughout the woods.

Nearing the end of seven months, the game was still going on. The woods were now covered in snow. One night, Edward realized that he was tired, beleaguered, worn out. His tent was cold. His socks and shoes were wet. He wanted a nice meal in a fine restaurant. In fact he was thinking about an excellent oyster stew he'd once had in a port town.

Just then a boy named Augustus flapped open Edward's tent flap and told him that he'd overheard some children from the Brothers Grimm camp talking about stories. 'It was about a boy and a girl getting lost in the woods. And there was another about a girl in a red hood, a short cut and a wolf. And another about a golden goose! They say that the stories are better than the game!'

'Stories?' Edward repeated, touching a hole in the knees of his trousers. 'I haven't heard a good story in ages! Who's telling the stories?'

'The Brothers Grimm!'

'Where?'

'By their campfire.'

Edward crawled out of his tent – it wasn't very tall and he was tired of crawling too. He stood up in the cold dusk and gave a loud whistle. His band of children came running from all directions. He waited until they were all there, standing before him.

'The game is over!' he announced.

The children were confused.

One said, 'But I think we can win this!'

Another said, 'We've almost got them!'

There was an uproar of grumbling.

Edward raised his hand to quiet them down. 'They have something better than the game. They have *stories*!'

'Stories?'

Edward dipped back into his tent, pulled out his pillowcase, tied it to a stick and waved it in the air. 'We're surrendering, but only on one condition.' He paused. 'We will demand stories!'

'Stories!' the children shouted.

And so Edward led the children across the woods, into Brothers Grimm territory. There they found them, all gathered round the fire. Wilhelm saw the white flag of surrender. Jacob was telling a story about a boy named Tom Thumb – who was extremely small – and so Wilhelm nodded to Edward, accepting his surrender, and waved him and his band of players to circle round the fire and listen.

For seven more months, there were stories. Stories upon stories upon stories, a feast of them! And it didn't matter that Edward was a grown man. The stories were thrilling. He loved them like he was a child again – like the lullaby stories that were found inside of his mother's tuba music each night. And one day, many years from this day, he would think of how important the Brothers Grimm's fairy tales were to him. He would find himself on a bicycle ride with his good friend C. S. Lewis, whom folks called Jack, and Jack's brother, Warny. They were on their way to the zoo. Edward was telling him the story of the Great Capture the Flag Game and the Brothers Grimm and their magical tales. Warny would shout across to Edward that perhaps he was too old for fairy tales, but Jack would interrupt. 'Some day you'll be old enough to start reading fairy tales again, Warny! Some day.' Fairy tales are for all of us, really – the best ones, at least – like C. S. Lewis's stories about a place called Narnia!

The fairy tales from the Brothers Grimm reminded Edward of the way he felt when he was a little boy with his hands cupped to the Aviary window – which is the same way that I felt when Bellini told me the stories of Magorium. Now, once again, there was a tingling in his hands and whirring in his chest and breaking open of his imagination! What was Edward's way in the world going to be? He still didn't know, but it seemed exciting, suddenly, to be ready to find it again!

And then one night the Brothers Grimm said, 'That's it! That's all we have!'

'You should write those down,' Edward told them.

'Do you think so?' Wilhelm asked.

'I do.'

'Maybe you're right,' Jacob said. 'We should go and write them down now.'

And so they broke up the camp and did just that.

Edward went back to the house of the Brothers Grimm. They were now hard at work, writing (which, I can tell you, seems a lot like sitting around and not doing much, but is actually hard work). And Edward worked alongside them. He jotted notes and sketches of new toys in his Book of Little Ideas. In fact, he jotted so many that he could no longer call it his Book of Little Ideas. It was now quite clearly a Medium-Sized Book of Medium-Sized Ideas.

He worked very hard, designing new toys so that he could go to:

GRENCHEN, SWITZERLAND – HOSTING THE NATIONAL SWISS TOY FAIR

Edward shuffled the remaining Jernklin dolls to one side of his trunk and filled the rest with his inventions. He headed off to the National Toy Fair which was being held in Switzerland. (Edward loved Switzerland, citing their favourable winter weather, superior hot chocolate and all the excess watch parts a young inventor could ever hope for!)

However, when he set up his booth and people started shuffling by, he realized that each of his designs looked like remakes of the Jernklin dolls or rehashed versions of the toy soldiers or things that he knew had already been invented. Although people were charmed by his tales of tubas and wings and Napoleon and the Great Capture the Flag Game, people weren't impressed by his toys. They oohed and aaahed at other booths, but were fairly quiet at his. He knew that he had to invent something new, something truly amazing, but he seemed to be lacking one thing: inspiration! (One day, years from this day, he would remember this moment while hunting for gold in Alaska with his good friend Jack London, who wrote a lot of books, including one you just may have heard of, *The Call of the Wild*. Jack would readjust his earmuffs and tell him that you can't wait for inspiration. You have to go after it with a club. And although Edward wasn't the type to go after things with clubs, necessarily, he agreed with Jack about inspiration, and always had.)

And after the fair, he set out, once again, to find some inspiration for his toys while looking for his way in the world.

HOLDERFIELD AND THE BAND OF PIRATES

Edward Magorium had never sailed the high seas. All of his brothers and sisters had – as a roving expert in the great Lipless Amazonian Lizard or while on tour as the Amphibious Frog Magoriums or the High-Flying Aeronautical Magoriums or while convention-hopping as a leading cosmetic dentistry innovator. Maybe he would find his way in the world by ship!

Edward didn't want to sail the high seas as a passenger, catching sun in a fancy tall hat and stiff cravat. No, no. He wanted to sail the high seas as a real sailor would, which was a good thing since he didn't have the money to book passage on a fancy ship (or, for that matter, to buy a tall hat and stiff cravat).

With no experience, he was dismissed by all of the ships except for one: *The Ballyhoo*. Edward didn't know it, but *The Ballyhoo* was actually a ship of pirates, led by a captain named Holderfield. Once they set sail and the dock was just a far-off dot, Magorium felt a little queasy and sat down on his trunk.

Just then Holderfield shouted from the helm, 'Press your knives to his throat, men, steal all of his belongings and make him walk the plank!' He glared at Edward, baring his teeth (which were actually quite pearly), and then, as if a little embarrassed by his outburst, he brushed some lint off his jacket. Edward noticed that the pirate's hand was shaking nervously. Was Holderfield nervous?

Edward surely was. He glanced around at the pirates on the deck. He didn't want to walk the plank and be eaten by sharks! The pirates were fumbling for their knives.

'Has anyone seen my knife?' one asked.

Edward looked at them pleadingly.

One said, 'He's looking at us pleadingly! I hate it when they do that!'

Another shouted back up to Holderfield. 'He's looking at us pleadingly! What should we do?'

Holderfield covered his face with his hand and shook his head wearily. 'Can't we just rob and kill one person! For once!'

Luckily for Edward, Holderfield was a bad pirate – by which I don't mean he was a mean pirate. No, no. I mean he was bad at being a pirate. He wasn't very weathered or appropriately wizened. His beard never really grew in. He had all of his limbs – no menacing hook arm or peg leg. He had both of his eyes, too, so no need for a patch. He'd tried a fake eye patch but it made him feel a little dizzy to only see out of one eye. He was allergic to birds and so even a parrot was out of the question.

His band of pirates were also bad pirates. They were always cordial, very well-mannered and tender-hearted. None of them really liked to drink grog. More than a few had been to hoity-toity private boarding schools.

Basically, none of the pirates had problems over-enunciating their Rs.

Edward looked around. *The Ballyhoo* was ancient and decrepit, but the plank looked almost new, as if it had never been used.

'Look,' Edward said, 'I don't think you should kill me. I mean, first of all, I'll give you my belongings

– except for this one book which is a kind of diary of ideas . . .'

'Pirates don't use the word *diary*,' one of the pirates said. 'We prefer the term *journal* or *log*. They're more manly.'

'Um, OK,' Edward said. 'I can give you everything else. It's a trunk of dolls. Not many left. But you can have them. They're Wonder Dolls, actually.'

'He has dolls!' one of the pirates shouted to Holderfield.

'Pirates don't play with dolls!'

'He says they're Wonder Dolls!'

'They change expressions along with the moods of their owners. They're magical,' Edward explained.

'He says they're magical!'

'Fine,' Holderfield said. 'Take the dolls. Then please press a knife to his throat and make him walk the plank. I paid good money for that plank!'

'Actually,' Edward said, 'I think I can be of use! I'm very inventive. I could help in some way, somehow. I'm sure of it!'

By this point, a bunch of pirates had gathered round the trunk, waiting to see the dolls.

'Can we look at the dolls now?' one of the pirates asked Holderfield.

'OK, OK,' he sighed.

For the next few days, the pirates became engrossed in the dolls. It turned out that they loved dolls. Dolls had been lacking in their lives. There was a doll meant just for Holderfield too. It had only a patchy beard, no eye patch, no peg leg or hook arm, but it did have one shaky hand.

The pirates were so engrossed in their dolls that they didn't notice a storm a-brewing.

Edward noticed the dark clouds, the gusty wind. 'Is there a storm coming?' he asked Holderfield.

'You get used to storms!' one of the pirates said, obviously tired of storms.

But this was a huge storm, and they let the ship dawdle right into the middle of it. The high seas grew very high. The ship was tossed around. The sky was ripped open by bolts of lightning. The rain poured down in sheets. The ship started to take on water. Edward and the crew were flung about. A few dolls were lost overboard, but no pirates.

Finally the ship was shoved to the shore, and they were shipwrecked.

Beaten, tired, waterlogged, half-drowned and now sandy, Edward felt sorry for himself for a moment. He truly did. And many years from this moment he would think back to this beaten, tired, waterlogged, half-drowned and sandy moment while thumb-wrestling his good friend Helen Keller. Helen was signing – because she couldn't speak – about self-pity actually. She said that self-pity is our worst enemy and, if we give in to it, we can never do anything good in the world. Luckily, Edward didn't feel sorry for himself for very long, because he had a lot of good left to do in the world!

Holderfield and the band of pirates and Edward found themselves stranded on the Isle of Wild Goats.

How did they know that it was the Isle of Wild Goats?

Hint 1: It was an island.

Hint 2: There were wild goats everywhere.

For the most part, the pirates loved being shipwrecked! (As I mentioned before, they were bad pirates and seemed to get everything wrong.) They built huts, took in the sun and enjoyed the cool blue water. There was plenty to eat and drink – if you liked goat and goat milk, which they did. Edward tied a net to two stakes and made up a game of two teams – one on either side of the net – popping a coconut over the net without letting it fall to the sand. It was a huge hit. (Many years later, while at a cocktail party in Holyoke, Massachusetts, he would tell this shipwreck story to a small enraptured group. One of whom, a physical education director who worked at a YMCA, became intrigued with this part, right here. It would break open his imagination, and in a few short months, he'd refine the idea – with a ball not a coconut – and he'd call it Mintonette – which isn't as catchy as its name now: Volleyball.)

Because life was so good, they worked half-heartedly on the ship.

The only person who didn't like being shipwrecked was Holderfield. It turns out that he was a pirate because he could only get a really good night's sleep while at sea. The rocking motion reminded him of his nursery and his loving nanny, Miss Fitchum. (He confessed this to Edward one evening, standing on the shore, among a small herd of wild goats, in a fit of tears. He added, 'Here I am, crying about my nanny. I'm a lousy pirate. I don't even have a parrot clamped to my shoulder!')

'I think I can help you, Holderfield,' Edward said. 'I have an idea.'

Now, if you're a vegetarian with deep feelings about animal rights – especially one who's not yet been shipwrecked on the Isle of Wild Goats – or another Isle filled with animals – then you might be very disturbed by Edward's plan. He'd read in an old book, years earlier, while at the Magorium School of Questions and Close Observation, that the Persians used to sleep on these strange beds of water. How? Edward recalled that they used goatskins, stitched together and filled with water. Goatskins, of all things!

Well, they'd eaten a few goats by now and hadn't had any purpose for their skins. And so, with the help of some pirates, Edward stitched together goatskins in the shape of a mattress and then he filled the mattress not with feathers, but with water. He called it the Bed of Sea Water. (Many years later, while hanging out in Haight-Ashbury in the 1960s, during Magorium's hippy phase – my, my, was he adored by hippies! – he would tell this shipwreck story to a small enraptured group. One of whom became intrigued with this part, right here. It would break open his imagination and, in a few short months, the waterbed, as we know it today, would be born in all of its groovy glory!)

Edward presented the Bed of Sea Water to Holderfield a week later. 'Here,' he said, 'now you can sleep on land, but feel like you're at sea.' He didn't say 'and being rocked by your loving nanny, Miss Fitchum'. Holderfield did still have some dignity left.

Holderfield was astonished. He lay down on the bed. He said, 'Oh, thank you! Thank you! Thank y–' And he fell fast asleep.

Eventually, some of the pirates decided to stay on the Isle of Goats, but others set sail again – including Holderfield at the helm, his Bed of Water in his private quarters. He was so thankful to Edward that he took him straight to his destination.

Where did Edward want to go?

Well, a few years back, he'd met a young author in a coffee shop in London. The man was complaining about a book of his that had been a failure. It was called *Moby Dick*. Edward had told the man not to worry. 'Maybe people don't understand how wonderful it is. Maybe they will figure it out one day.' The man had been so grateful for the kind words, he pulled a copy of the book out of his bag and inscribed it. It read: *For you, Edward Magorium. A true inspiration! Remember that life is a journey that's homeward bound!* And he signed it: *Herman Melville.* Edward had always remembered it, and now he wanted to go home.

When they arrived on land, Edward had a parting gift for Holderfield. 'This is for you,' Edward said. 'Because a real pirate needs a parrot.'

Edward had fashioned a stuffed animal, painted it bright colours, and given it stiff claws that could pinch a shoulder and stay put. (He did this work alongside a pirate named Charlie who loved making the stuffed bird and later opened a shop in London called Charlie's Stuffed Creatures for Children.)

When Holderfield held the stuffed parrot, he teared up once more – as did all of the other pirates who were saying farewell. (They were all so tender-hearted.)

'Here,' Holderfield said. 'I should pay you for all your work as a fine sailor and for the things you've given us.' He reached into the pocket of his waistcoat.

'No, no,' Edward said. 'It was my pleasure.' And, years from this moment, Edward would remember this teary goodbye while being taught how to play Chopsticks on the organ by his good friend Albert Schweitzer, and Albert would tell him that even if it's just a little thing that you do, you should do something for others – something that you don't get paid for except for the privilege of doing it. And

Edward felt privileged for having given Holderfield his Bed of Sea Water and his stuffed parrot.

'We will miss you, Magorium! We will miss you terribly,' Holderfield said, and then he clamped a clean, folded, freshly ironed handkerchief to his nose, as did the other pirates – because they were all bad pirates but very well-mannered.

I think we should move on.

Jernklin — sad, mournful, but beautiful death of . . .

When Edward arrived home, he spent time with his parents. His father observed him closely and asked many questions. 'Have you been eating enough? Do you need a new suit? Have you found your way in the world?'

Edward answered as best as he could. 'Yes, yes, no.'

His mother played the tuba for them, a beautiful oompah tune she'd written herself. (She once asked herself why she didn't compose music, and because she couldn't come up with a good answer, she started composing.)

Edward heard all about his siblings. Ansgar had just given a talk to a national scientific academy of some sort on the Lipless Amazonian Lizard's communication skills. He'd evidently learned to speak their language. The Amphibious Frog Magoriums and the Flying Aeronautical Magoriums were both touring in the new country – the United States of America. And Ulrika was making new teeth for royalty.

His brothers and sisters' lives seemed so clear, and Edward still hadn't found his way in the world. He needed to visit Jernklin.

When Edward got to Jernklin's shop, a young woman was sweeping up the shop. She told Edward that Jernklin was in the hospital and that he was very sick. Edward ran to the hospital, and found Jernklin sleeping in a narrow bed, facing a window that overlooked a garden. He'd aged. His hair was a finer wisp of white and propped on his bedside table was his own Jernklin doll, whose hair was also a finer wisp of white.

Edward sat down and waited for Jernklin to wake up.

'I've been waiting for you,' Jernklin said, when he opened his eyes.

'You have?'

'Tell me, what have you been doing? Where have you gone? What's your way in the world?'

Edward told him everything about Napoleon, the Brothers Grimm, the pirates. He even updated him on the lives of the people in his family, because at least they had found their ways in the world. It took a long time, and when he was finished, he said, 'So, as you can see, I haven't found my way in the world. I've just gone on, not inventing anything new. I'm sorry.'

'Edward,' Jernklin said. 'You've given gifts of yourself! You've inspired those around you! You are finding your way in the world! This is it!'

'It is?' Edward asked.

Jernklin nodded. 'It is.'

Edward sat with Jernklin every day. Edward would ask Jernklin what he thought Edward might invent one day, but Jernklin didn't answer. He didn't seem to care. He would only say, 'Look out of the window, Edward. Look at that beautiful sky! It's a simple pleasure, and simplest pleasures are the most precious.'

They spent a lot of time just looking out of the window.

Jernklin slept most of the time. And then the day

came when Jernklin closed his eyes, went to sleep and didn't wake up. He was smiling, though, in his deep rest. Smiling. And the sun was on his face, and the birds were outside the window, chirping.

Edward placed the Jernklin doll in Jernklin's arms, and cried for a long while. It's hard to say goodbye to people you love.

Later, he went out into the garden, and he looked up into the sky. He was looking for a cloud in the shape of Jernklin or at least the foamy wisp of his hair, but he was distracted by a bluebird, skipping from branch to branch. He noticed that the bird didn't flap his wings very often. He used his small structure of bones and feathers to float or glide through the air. (Years and years later, Edward would think back to this moment in the garden while eating sweets – an odd and various and delicious assortment of oddly flavoured bonbons – with his good friend Roald Dahl. Roald was talking about the art of watching. With both cheeks packed with goodies, he said in a muffled voice that above all else you should watch with glittering eyes the whole world around you because the greatest secrets are always hidden in the most unlikely places.) Edward had given up on being a bird somewhere along the way. And he'd given up on watching birds as he once had at the Aviary window. But now he was watching them with glittering eyes – and he felt a tingling in his hands, a whirring in his chest and a breaking open of his imagination. Edward thought of Leonardo da Vinci and the etchings about flight in his book, and he thought of his own etchings, the ones from his boyhood, the ones he used to show Jernklin, from time to time.

Edward ran to the nearest stationers and bought several reams of paper, thinking of Jernklin the whole time, thinking of how he didn't want to talk about inventions. He only wanted Edward to look at the sky!

He was frustrated at first. Very frustrated. He tried this and that and the other. Years later he would remember this moment of frustration late one night in Louis Pasteur's kitchen while dunking cookies in milk – pasteurized milk – and talking with him about life and such. Pasteur told him the secret to his success in reaching his goals. He told Edward that his strength lay solely in his tenacity – meaning that he just stuck to it – whatever it was. And, although Edward had yet to hear this secret, he must have had the same secret, because he didn't give up! And, in the end, he had a new invention! A simple invention that gave simple pleasure, which is the most precious kind!

KALAMARIA – NATIONAL TOY FAIR OF GREECE

This time Edward set up a booth at the National Toy Fair and he only advertised one product: Mr Magorium's Creased Contraptions of Gossamer Aviation. And his toy was not for sale. In fact, the children had to make it themselves.

Edward handed them a piece of paper. Only that. He taught them how to fold it this way and that, that way and this until they had in their hands what is known today as the paper aeroplane.

The paper aeroplane stunned crowds and delighted children, and the fact that he would take no money, this act of generosity, struck some as foolhardy, but proved genius. The paper aeroplane became an international phenomenon!

For years there would be much debate over

the origin of the paper aeroplane, but those at the National Toy Fair of Greece in Kalamaria that year knew exactly where they began: inside the brain of Edward Magorium!

They awarded Edward Magorium the highest honour: Toymaker of the Year. (And actually they used the word *toymaker* even though they were Greeks speaking Greek, because, oddly enough, the word for toymaker in Greek is *toymaker*.)

He won the award seventeen more times in a row.

Living the High Life

Maybe you've been wondering all this time how it was that Edward was going to come to meet all of these good friends that he ended up having over the course of his life.

Well, it happened right about now like this:

Edward became a famous toymaker and the requests came pouring in. He created toys on commission for international dignitaries, celebrities and various notables. To have a one-of-a-kind Magorium toy became all the rage in the 19th century.

For example:

During a reading tour in New York City in 1867, Charles Dickens invited Edward for tea, telling him that he'd buy any toy that he brought with him. Edward brought him small doll replicas of his books' heroes – David Copperfield, Oliver Twist and Scrooge. But he also invented a new kind of ink just for Dickens. He put it in a bottle of thick shoe polish – one he found from Warren's Boot-Blacking Factory where Charles had worked for years, starting out as a twelve-year-old boy, pasting labels on shoe-polish jars ten hours a day. Charles Dickens picked up the jar in his shaking hands. Dickens was older now, but still had a curly beard and those sad downward-sloping eyebrows.

'Where did you find this?' he asked.

'It took some looking,' Edward said. 'Open it up. Dip a pen into it. Write a word. It's Magical Magorium Ink.'

Dickens did just that. He wrote the word Magorium on a piece of paper. Although the ink looked black and Dickens had written Magorium in small letters in the middle of the page, the word Magorium expanded across the page in bright reds and blues and greens like a sunburst.

This was so moving to Dickens that his eyes brimmed with tears. 'This is my life,' he said to Edward. 'Starting from this small tub of polish and wildly filling the page.'

*　　*　　*

And for another example:

For Robert Louis Stevenson, he made a commemorative set of spillikins, which is the old-fashioned variety of Pick Up Sticks, but in the old game the sticks were carved into the shapes of weapons. But for Stevenson, Magorium shaped them into pens, of course. And he fashioned a doll with two faces – a normal one for Dr Jekyll, a terrifying one for Mr Hyde.

And another example:

Magorium was commissioned by Charles Darwin to make toys for his ten children. Magorium made Evolvo-Creatures – beetles that turned into butterflies, earthworms that became eagles, frogs that became French pastry chefs.

And another example:

He was called upon to make a toy for a young British girl's birthday. Her name was Beatrix. He told the girl's father that he'd have to meet her first so that he would know the perfect gift. Beatrix and Magorium had tea together and then headed off on a walk under the watchful eye of the governess, following behind.

'Hurry up,' Beatrix said. 'I think we can lose her.'

'OK,' said Magorium.

And they walked faster and faster until the governess was just a voice calling after her.

'Why are we running?' Magorium asked.

'Fungus,' Beatrix answered.

Edward had no idea what she was talking about.

They stopped at a shady spot in the woods, and Beatrix began explaining all that she'd learned by looking at mushrooms, and lichen crawling up trees, and algae collected on rocks. 'It's all very alive,' she said, and she showed him her notebook (she had a book of ideas too!), and translated it from the secret coded language she'd invented. 'My parents have appointed me housekeeper. They don't want me to study and to have a scientific life. My uncle tried to get me accepted into the Royal Botanical Gardens at Kew, but they wouldn't let me enter, because I'm a girl. It's very unfair. Don't you think?'

Edward agreed. 'It is,' he said. 'Very unfair.'

Just then a small rabbit hopped by. Beatrix said, 'My parents would like you to make me a stuffed rabbit or something, I suppose,' she said. 'But now you know that what I really love is fungus.'

By now Edward had known enough great thinkers to understand that young Beatrix Potter was training her eye for some great adventure in life.

He sent her a stuffed rabbit, wearing a blue jacket with small brass buttons, which made her parents very happy. But he also attached a note to Beatrix, written in her secret code, and it explained what was hidden inside of the rabbit – a science kit, complete with a microscope for the closer investigation of the world!

The most important request, however – the one that truly changed Magorium's way of thinking about toys – came from the . . .

MANCHU QING DYNASTY

Empress Dowager Cixi called Magorium to China to build a true one-of-a-kind Magorium toy for her nephew Guangxu – who'd been emperor almost since his birth. He was now three years old. Magorium had an unlimited budget and took a ship to China where he stayed for many months working on just this single toy. Magorium would refer to his time in China as truly wondrous, citing the rich colours, the honourable people and the adoration of dragons, although he was confounded as to why a culture with so many available noodles would refuse to suck them.

After much time and slavish work, Mr Magorium finally finished the toy. What remains intriguing about this story is that all the details of the toy itself have been lost, and this is why:

The toy was presented to the Emperor as soon as he awoke for his birthday. The family – including his feisty aunt – priests, diplomats and guards, and Magorium himself stood around as the little emperor peeled the wrapping paper away, opened the lid and the toy was removed. Everyone gasped. The Empress Dowager Cixi, who was really in control of everything, knelt before him and praised him for his brilliance. A priest fainted.

And then the little boy put the toy aside and for the next several hours . . . played with the box!

Humiliation washed over the palace. The little emperor didn't pay any attention to the miraculous toy.

Magorium sat down and watched the child in awe. He saw something that no one else could see. The toy – despite its exquisite design and ingenuity – could only be that, a toy. The box, however, could be anything the little emperor imagined.

He wrote to his good friend Mark Twain, 'What a fool I've been. It isn't the toys we love. It's the inspiration the toys give us. That's what fills us with joy! The greatest toy cannot surpass the brilliance of even the simplest mind!'

From then on, he no longer focused on the imagination of his own mind (although he'd always dabble). Instead he concentrated on inspiring the inspiration of others, mostly children, and his Book of Medium-Sized Ideas became his Book of Big Ideas – which Bellini would take over for him, as biographer, as notationist. The Big Book became the Big Book, however, in this very moment, when Edward finally understood his way in the world.

Isn't this what Jernklin had been trying to teach him? He hadn't just been educating him on the knotty joints of dolls. No, no. He'd been trying to make him understand this selflessness. 'You have to remove yourself,' he'd told Edward. Isn't this what Edward had done as a child, really? Hadn't he inspired his father and mother to ask hard questions? Hadn't he inspired Ansgar, Bernd, Brunhild, Walburga, Rambert and Ulrika?

Years and years from this moment in time, after years and years of concentrating on the imaginations of others, Magorium would find himself on a horseback ride with the famous Will Rogers.

Feeling a bit low, Will said to him, 'Heroing is one of the shortest-lived professions there is.'

'But making other people heroes?' Magorium asked.

Will Rogers thought about that for a moment. 'There's a career that might have staying power.'

Never-ending list of people inspired by Edward Magorium (the abridged version, of course, because the never-ending version would be never-ending!) and not in any particular order!

THOMAS EDISON – FINALLY! – THE WIZARD OF MENLO PARK

Edward Magorium spent many rainy afternoons in the cosy parlour of Thomas Edison – locked in epic battles of noughts-and-crosses. (Young Edison was a master of noughts-and-crosses.)

One rainy day in particular, they were in a heated competition, sitting in front of the fire without any lights on. No one had any lights on, actually, because Thomas Edison hadn't invented lightbulbs yet. (No one had any record players, because he hadn't invented those either. Nor had he improved the telephone so really there wasn't much to do on rainy days. In fact, although more than a century had passed since the Age of Enlightenment, you'd be surprised at how itchy, woolly and stinky things still were.)

In a moment of panic, Edison put an O in a bad spot, and Edward won the game easily with diagonal Xs.

'Will you look at that?' Edison fumed. He slumped in his chair and ran his hands through his hair. 'I'm just not thinking very clearly,' he said to Edward. He leaned forward and suddenly looked like he might cry. 'I haven't had a good idea in ages. I had a school teacher once who thought my brains were scrambled! Sometimes I feel like I'm only failing without taking any steps forward!'

'Failing without taking steps forward? That's not possible,' Edward said loudly. (He said everything loudly to Thomas Edison because he was hard of hearing.)

'I get all of my best ideas when I'm falling asleep,' Edison continued, 'but then I'm asleep and so they drift away.'

'Fixable,' said Edward Magorium. 'Completely

fixable! You just need to trap the ideas before they drift away.'

'Trap them?'

'You need an idea trap!' Edward said, standing up and searching the room for things he might need.

'An idea trap?' Edison repeated.

'We'll also need a cage to put the ideas in once you've trapped them,' Edward said. 'Do you have a Book of Little Ideas – or Medium-Sized Ideas or even Big Ideas?'

'I have a book where I put my notes, yes.'

'OK, then.'

Edward sent Edison to the kitchen to get pie pans while he went off to the garage to get ball bearings. They met back in the parlour near the fireplace.

'How is this going to help?' Edison asked.

'Where do you do your falling asleep and best idea making?'

'Here in this chair, staring into the fire.'

He sat Edison down in the chair, put a ball bearing in each of his hands and pie pans below. He put Edison's Book of Medium-Sized Ideas on a side table with a bottle of ink and a pen. (Edison's book would also become quite a BIG BOOK.)

Edward grabbed his hat and his coat. He said, 'I'm off now. Must run.'

'But, but, I don't understand. What am I supposed to do now?'

'Stare into the fire. That's all.'

Edward then left.

Edison sat there. He stared into the fire. He thought big thoughts – perhaps about things like record players and telephones and lightbulbs – and when his mind went dreamy, a brilliant idea began lurking at the edges of his mind, lumbering along like a bear – and Edison kept getting dreamier and dreamier until he started to fall asleep and lose the brilliant idea again. But then because he was so sleepy, his hands relaxed. The ball bearings slipped from his palms and rattled the pie pans below.

He jolted awake, grabbed his book and his pen and jotted down his brilliant idea. From then on he had brilliant ideas all the time.

And that, my friends, is why I am writing this in a lit room.

ISADORA DUNCAN

After the San Francisco earthquake, Magorium found himself in the crumbled city. He brought with him gears, wires, hammers, nails, paint sets, glue, ice-lolly sticks – everything kids might want to rebuild their lost toys – and, of course, paper to teach kids how to fold aeroplanes.

While at an ice-cream parlour, he met a girl named Isadora Duncan. They sat at the counter together. Magorium tried to interest her in inventing a new toy, in rebuilding.

She leaned forward and whispered, 'I'm afraid that the earthquake is inside me now. I think I may have swallowed some of it, and it's here to stay.'

Magorium thought about this. 'Well, that was smart of you.'

'Smart of me? To swallow part of the earthquake?' the girl asked.

'I think that another word for an earthquake inside you might be dance! Do you like to dance?' He'd noticed the girl had kept moving her toes on the floor in miniature dance steps the whole time they'd been sitting there.

'I do,' she said. 'I like my own way of dancing.'

'Then do it your own way,' he said.

She became the Mother of Modern Dance. I don't know how someone gives birth to something like dance, but she did. Modern dance is a kind of dance that isn't all pointed toes and delicate hands, which is to say that she continued to do it her own way.

CLAUDE MONET

Once, while on a train heading to Paris, Edward sat next to a man with paint caught in his fingernails. He asked the man if he was an artist.

'I used to be,' the man said. 'And a well-known one too. But I'm finished with all of that now.' The man looked quite sad. His eyes had gone teary and he stared out of the window.

'Why are you finished?' Magorium asked.

'My eyesight's gone. Everything is blurry. I've lost my true vision.'

Magorium thought about that for a moment, the train car rattling down the track. They disappeared into a tunnel, and when they came out to the brightness on the other side, Magorium said to the man, 'You've lost one kind of vision, but you've gained another.'

'I have?'

'You should paint what you see!' he said. 'It's true because you see it as the truth.'

And so now we have the blurry paintings of Claude Monet – quite impressionistic!

Jackie Robinson

When Magorium found himself in Pasadena, California, he decided to meet a gang. He'd never met a gang before, and he wondered if they wouldn't like to do something other than be gang-ish.

He was expecting a group of thugs, but what he found was a group of kids. Kids in gangs are just kids after all.

The Pepper Street Gang had a new member named Jackie. Magorium asked him if he'd like to do something other than being gang-ish.

'Like what?' Jackie asked.

'Like using your imagination, like inventing something.'

'I don't have time for that,' Jackie said.

'Everyone has time for that,' Magorium said.

'What do you know about everyone?'

'True,' Magorium said. There was no way he could know about everyone. In fact, no one can know about everyone. 'Why don't you have time for that?'

'My mother irons people's clothes all day long for a living. She's got six kids. My father is long gone. She's barely keeping food on the table. I work, too, making money when I can. And, if I have to steal food, I steal it.' He looked at Magorium as if challenging him. Magorium didn't. He'd gone through a lean time in Paris when the Jernklin dolls weren't selling, and he'd stolen food himself. Jackie was lean and strong. His skin was a rich dark colour, his eyes fast and sharp. When he saw that Magorium wasn't going to tell him that stealing food was wrong, the way some other people might, Jackie went on. 'All the white people in our neighbourhood signed a petition to get us kicked out of the neighbourhood. Do you think that was easy for my mother?'

'No, I don't,' Magorium said.

'She stood her ground, though. She stood her ground.'

'And you?' Magorium said. 'Are you always going to stand your ground?'

'I am,' Jackie said.

'You want to make sure of one thing, though,' Magorium said.

'What's that?'

'That you know how to use your imagination, that you know how to invent.'

'I told you that I don't have time for that,' Jackie said. 'I just explained it to you.'

'It always comes back to imagination and

invention,' Magorium said. 'You have to first imagine a better world before you can begin to invent it and only then can you build it.'

Jackie stared at him for a moment. He let that idea sink in, and then he smiled. 'You and me. We agree on this, don't we? I think we're on the same team.'

'Yep,' Magorium said. 'I think we are.'

ROBERT FROST

Once Magorium was playing tag with a group of kids in the woods of Massachusetts. There, he came across a boy who'd just moved from the west coast. The boy didn't know anyone and was lurking at the edges of the game.

Magorium walked up to him, and talked to him for a bit. 'Why aren't you playing tag?'

'I'm not sure,' the boy said, looking up at the limbs of a birch tree.

'Would you rather make something up? Some other game?'

The boy shrugged. He was quiet with pale blue eyes.

'If you could make up a game, what would it be?' Magorium asked.

'Those birches,' the boy said. 'They look good for

swinging, like you could get a good jump and maybe even touch the sky. Don't they?'

Magorium hadn't ever considered swinging in birches. 'Yes, yes,' he said. 'They surely do.'

And so they started swinging in the birches and the other kids joined in too.

Bobby Frost went on to write poems, famous ones, and one, in particular, called 'Birches', which he sent to good old Magorium with the inscription, *'Happiness makes up in height what it lacks in length! I was happy swinging from birches!'*

Mahatma Gandhi

Magorium set sail for India. He'd never been. He wanted to know what games the children of India played.

While there he got caught up in a game of kabaddi, which entails holding your breath, running and shoving. The game got a little rough, and soon enough a shoving match broke out between the two teams.

One of the boys walked off and sat down by a tree.

Magorium followed him. 'What's wrong?' he asked.

'I don't understand why they have to fight each time like that,' the boy said.

'Why don't you tell them not to?'

'What good would that do?'

'I don't know,' Magorium said. 'But it's worth a try.'

And so the little boy stood and walked back to the game. He started speaking to the crowd of fighting children. He didn't shout. He spoke in a quiet voice about peace, and slowly, one by one, the kids began to listen. Finally, no one was fighting.

The boy stopped speaking, and all of the kids stared at each other, a little embarrassed, a little unsure of what to do next.

'Now, let's start again,' the boy said.

And they did.

The boy's name was Gandhi. He never stopped talking about peace. He became a great leader, and eventually was called Mahatma meaning 'Great Soul', and, because he became the Father of India, people called him Bapu, which means father. And who wouldn't want the nickname Bapu?

ELVIS PRESLEY

Edward Magorium toured the South, and while in Tupelo, Mississippi – known for its tupelo trees

– reading comic books in a drugstore, a boy walked up and started reading right beside him. The boy's mother was never far off. She kept darting back to see if her son was OK.

And when he told her that he was doing just fine and that she didn't have to dote on him like that, Edward noticed the boy's stutter, but didn't mention it.

They ended up talking about comic-book heroes. The boy's name was Elvis, and he had shiny hair, slicked back, except for a forelock that fell into his eyes.

When it was about time to go, he said, 'Y-y-you're OK in my b-b-book. I d-d-don't have much in f-f-friends. B-b-but I like you. B-b-because you don't make f-f-fun of my stutter or my m-m-mama, who's always right with m-m-me.'

Magorium was used to stuttering. He'd known many stutterers – Churchill, the little Emperor Guangxu, even Napoleon had occasionally stammered a bit, especially when furious and he was often furious. He'd read that his beloved Sir Isaac Newton and Aristotle had stuttered too. And then there was Teddy Roosevelt – for whom he'd made some teddy bears – and an acquaintance of his, Lewis Carroll, who'd written *The Adventures of Alice in Wonderland* and that poem that never made any sense called 'Jabberwocky'. (Not to mention that rascal, Ty Cobb, who was the most viciously competitive draughts player Magorium had ever met!)

'Do you stutter when you sing?' Edward asked the boy, because he'd heard that this was not always the case.

'N-no,' Elvis said, thinking about it.

'Maybe you should sing more, then!' Edward said.

'M-m-maybe I should,' Elvis said.

And he did.

E. B. White

Magorium decided to make all of his musical instruments play in full colour. He'd been very lucky with the trumpet, and the tuba, of course, because of his childhood. The oboe had proven so impossible to reason with that he'd set it aside, and now he was on the hunt for the perfect piano to work with. And he wanted one that already had coloured keys so you could see what colour you were playing.

He headed to a piano manufacturing company and while waiting to talk to the boss, he met the boss's son who was also waiting. He was a stuffed-up boy with a terribly runny nose and a balled-up wad of tissues in his hand.

'How are you feeling?' Magorium asked him.

'Allergic. I feel allergic to mostly everything.'

'Like what?'

'Like things you can't even really see.'

'Do you believe in things you can't even really see?' Magorium asked.

The boy nodded and then whispered. 'I'm scared most of all of things that can't be seen.'

'Like what?'

'Well, I don't like the dark because you can't see anything in it. I don't like the end of summer, which you can't see.'

'Are you afraid of things you *can* see?'

'I don't like the bathrooms in the school basement, and I'm afraid of having to speak in front of crowds.' Then the boy's face brightened. 'But we're going to Maine in a few days for the entire summer and I can breathe there and there's no basement bathroom and no one is going to ask me to give any kind of speech. It's a good thing my last name is White. The school year usually ends before they get to the end of the alphabet and so I don't have to give my speech.'

Just then the boy leaned down to a corner of the warehouse where a small spider was making a web between the wall and one of the packing boxes. 'Look at that!' he said.

'Amazing!' Magorium said.

'That spider must be very wise,' the boy said. 'That's a very complicated web, isn't it?'

'Very wise. We should ask her questions, important ones, about life. That's what I always do when I meet someone who's very wise.'

The boy stood up stiffly and looked Magorium in the eye. 'She can't talk,' he said flatly.

'You believe in things you can't quite see, but not in things you can't quite hear?' Magorium asked.

'Oh,' the boy said. 'I know what you're saying.'

'Of course she can talk. You just have to be an extremely good listener to hear her.'

The boy bent back down to the spider, and as Magorium walked into the boss's office to talk about pianos that play in full colour, he could hear the boy asking the spider questions.

Magorium decided that the boy must have figured out how to understand the language of spiders because, later, he grew up to be E. B. White and he wrote a book about a spider named Charlotte and her amazing web-work – perhaps you've heard of it?

BOBBY FISHER AND HIS SISTER

In May 1949, Magorium was buying a set of bonbons for his good friend Roald Dahl – who always wanted more bonbons and eventually went on to write a book about chocolate (and a boy named Charlie and a sweet-maker named Wonka) – and fell in line behind a girl who wanted to buy a game of chess.

She put her money on the counter and the cashier counted it out. 'Fifty cents shy,' he said. 'Sorry, kid. You'll have to put it back.'

'But I don't have fifty more cents,' the girl said, and then she scraped her money off the counter and shoved it in her pocket. She turned round, ready to put the box back on the shelf.

'I'll pay the extra fifty cents,' Magorium said, and then he turned to the girl. 'Under one condition.'

'What's that?'

'I'm sharing with you,' he said, 'my fifty cents. And so you will have to share the game with someone else.'

The girl's eyes darted around the store. 'Do I have to?'

'Don't you want to?'

'I don't want to share it with my brother, Bobby,' she said. 'If that's what you mean. I have to share everything with him!'

'Well, then, that's the condition. You have to share this game of chess with your brother, Bobby. That's the one and only condition!'

The girl looked down at her shoes then looked at the box in her arms. 'OK,' she said. 'A deal's a deal.'

And she was true to her word. It turned out that Bobby had a knack for chess. He read the instructions found in the chess set and eventually became the greatest player in the world of chess – which is a bigger world than you'd think!

ON AND ON

The Never-Ending List of People Inspired by Magorium IS TRULY never-ending. Bellini read me much of it on that rainy day, but not all of it. Not even close. I sat there hypnotized, drinking in as much as I could. Did I realize that the rain was easing up? Did I realize that my socks were drying out? No, I did not, because I was engrossed, and I would love to tell it ALL to you, every last drop. I'm doing the best I can, you know, to remember it all! But it DOES go on and on. I don't even know all of the stories myself.

But I do know that I can't go on and on. I have a compendium to finish, thank you very much!

Please

P lease, continue on!

Q – THE LETTER ITSELF

Q is a difficult letter. Have you ever noticed that very few words begin with the letter Q? Since that is the case, why don't you . . .

R ead on!

SHOES

Many of you may have noticed that Edward Magorium had an extremely long life – 243 years to be exact.

Some scientists say that it was his aerobic lifestyle. The Table Tennis Coalition claims that it was his love of table tennis that kept him so fit. The Marco Polo Swimming Game Association of America insists that it was his love of the game Marco Polo. The European Bocce Ball League claims that it was the calming effects of bocce ball on his heart that kept him alive. In fact, on the website of just about every sporty group – International Twister Association, Allied Frisbee Enthusiasts of New Zealand, Professional Pogo Stickers of the World, United Community of Yo-yo-ists, etc. etc. etc. – all claim that their sport had the greatest effect on his fine health. Maybe it was a combination?

Nutritionists claim that it was his innovative style of eating healthy foods which entailed a method of 'playing with his food at the table'. Generally frowned upon through the ages by parental types, it turns out that it may actually be an excellent way to get kids to eat vegetables. Someone is now at work on a research study.

Magorium himself couldn't explain other than to say this: 'I'm full of life, and I've also made a commitment to my shoes.'

Always frugal, Magorium didn't believe in wasting anything. Once, when he was in Vienna, he found a pair of shoes that fitted his feet perfectly. He bought a lifetime supply so he'd never be without them. He had to make a guess at his lifetime. He guessed a very long time – because he didn't want to come up short on shoes right near the end – and since he made the commitment, he stuck to it.

STORE, BIRTH OF MR MAGORIUM'S WONDER EMPORIUM

Edward Magorium had the perfect shoes, yes, but he was tired of following them to all the places they wanted to go. He didn't mind travel as much as he missed having a place to call home.

He didn't just need a home for himself either. He needed a home for all of his toys as well.

People live in homes. Toys live in toy stores.

Why not a building that was really both in one?

He thought about building a toy store with a home inside, but that didn't seem quite right. There were so many buildings who didn't have caretakers. Why build another one?

And so he set out to find the building that belonged to him – maybe a building that had been left behind – a building that needed him as much as he needed it.

He looked in city after city, in nook and cranny of city after city. He looked high and low, inside and out, far and wide. And then he remembered looking for Jernklin – all those many years ago as a boy in Luxembourg. He'd walked up and down every street he could find, and then he had to stop – to give Jernklin a chance to find him. That's what happened then. Maybe it would happen again.

And so he repeated everything he'd done before. He volunteered to sweep up bird feathers at a pet shop and a local zoo. He collected as many as he could. He then fashioned wings, gluing the feathers to cloth. He strapped them on and walked to a lush park early one morning. Once there, he waited for a breeze. The breeze came. He ran and flapped and ran and flapped. The wings caught a belch of air. He tipped ever so slightly off the ground and then came to a stumbling stop.

There was the cat. Not the same cat, of course – a completely different cat, but a cat just the same.

And Magorium took off running, the cat at his heels.

They ran and ran until Magorium lost the cat in a maze of streets, also getting lost himself.

He was dazed, dizzy, blurry-eyed. He looked up the street and down it. And then he looked up to see the sun, to get his bearings. He grew dizzier looking up like that, and fell to the kerb. There he lay, sprawled out this time, his gluey, feathery wings splayed at his back.

And that's when he saw the little FOR SALE sign, propped in a dusty window.

He stood up, wiped a spot on the glass and stared inside. It was empty. The shelves were blank. It would take careful tending, but it was beautiful. Quite perfect.

He walked up to the door, twisted the knob. It opened – as it had been waiting for him. The door hinges gave a little cry – like the cry of a newborn baby.

'My store,' Magorium said. 'I'll name you Mr Magorium's Wonder Emporium!'

The hinges stopped crying, and the store let out a contented sigh.

Magorium had found a place to call home.

Toys

And the toys? They burst on to the shelves. They darted up and down the rows. They twirled from the rafters – all to the sounds of the full-colour piano. Which is to say: they were happy to be home too!

Unusual (and sometimes unintended) Toy Inventions

The Moon Bounce

Magorium was waiting for a tennis lesson. He had an upcoming match with a fourteen-year-old girl named Billie Jean who would one day become a great tennis champion and leader in the feminist movement! She'd challenged him to a tennis duel, and he'd been foolish enough to take her up on it.

While he was waiting, he saw a man experimenting with an inflatable cover on a neighbouring court. The man, named Scurlock, was working very hard, trying to get his invention to work just so, but his employees were bouncing wildly on the inflatable thing, caught up in the fun of it. Scurlock was furious.

His face was flushed. Sweat had seeped across the back of his shirt.

Magorium walked up and peeked through the fencing. 'What have you got there?'

'A failed invention,' the man said. 'And a lousy crew of workers.'

'Look again,' Magorium said. 'I think you have invented something. Something delightful.'

Scurlock looked at his employees again, bouncing joyfully like a pack of kids at a birthday party.

'It's like walking on the moon!' one of the employees shouted.

Scurlock turned to Magorium to thank him, but Magorium was on his own court now, practising his wobbly serve. (He lost his match with Billie Jean – in straight sets.)

SILLY PUTTY

Poor James Wright was working to find a substitute for artificial rubber during World War Two. He came up with this odd, silly, bouncing, stringy compound. He sent it to researchers far and wide. None of them knew what to do with it – except for one.

Edward Magorium got his batch by accident. He lived next door to a researcher and the address label had been smeared by rain. Magorium may not have known how to use the strange substance to help the war effort, except in terms of morale. This stuff was fun to play with! Once he accidentally left a wad on some comic strips and then set a coffee mug down on top of it. When he pulled it up, there was Dagwood, one of his favourite characters, imprinted in the putty. He stretched Dagwood's face this way and that, that way and this.

He wrote James Wright a letter:

You have invented an amazing toy – like no other I've ever seen. Its purpose is clear: bouncing, twisting, cartoon distorting and general bloppy, stringy amusement! Congratulations!

But it's unclear whether Wright ever received the letter or if he simply tossed it out.

Dr Earl Warrick made a similar silicone bouncing putty, and finally Peter Hodgson went to a party where chemists – a lively group! – were playing with it. He decided it was a toy and came up with the name Silly Putty, because it is silly and it is putty.

THE HULA HOOP

Kids have played with hoops since the beginning of time. They've made them from grapevines and willow branches and tall grasses. Egyptian children rolled their hoops and hit them with sticks to keep them rolling – this was about, oh, 3,000 years ago! The Greeks used them in weight-loss regimens and in the 14th century, hoops were all the rage in England – so much so that they got blamed for heart failure, and 18th-century sailors decided that hooping was much like the hula dancers they'd seen in Hawaii and so that part of the name was added on.

Magorium was around when the modern plastic version of the hula hoop first popped up as an idea. He was hanging out with Richard Knerr and Arthur 'Spud' Melin, talking to them about their Wham-O catapult, which Magorium was using to shoot pieces of beef into the air to feed his pet falcon. They were talking about some friend of theirs who said that Australian children were swirling bamboo hoops in circles round their middles while in gym.

'Oh, yes,' Magorium said. 'I miss my old hooping days in England!'

'Is it fun?' Spud asked. 'Swirling a hoop?'

'Fun?' Magorium said. 'Why, it's hypnotic! Every child should have a hoop to call their own!'

And so the men set to it – and soon sold over 100

million hula hoops – one of which you've probably tried to swirl!

THE SLINKY

What was Magorium doing at the Cramp shipyards in Philadelphia one afternoon in the 1940s?

He was looking for spare parts for a Young Toy Inventors Convention, that's what!

And there he ended up sharing his peanut-butter-and-guava-jam sandwich with an engineer named Richard James. James's table was a bit of a mess and at one point a torsion spring fell off and rolled on the deck.

'Sorry about the mess,' Richard said.

'Not a problem,' Magorium told him. 'Actually, I'd like to see that again.'

'What?'

'That spring falling off the table and rolling on the deck.'

Richard picked it up, fiddled with it in his hands, passing it back and forth, and then set it up and sent it off the table.

'Well, I don't know much about being an engineer in a shipyard, but I do know one thing very well,' Magorium said.

'What's that?' Richard asked.

'I know a toy when I see one.'

That night Richard showed the spring to his wife Betty, and they set to work developing the toy.

Later that year, Magorium was in Gimbels in Philadelphia, meandering through the toy department where he saw a display of the Slinky – and its battery-free walking.

Working behind the display was Richard and his wife Betty. 'Magorium!' Richard shouted. 'It's a Slinky!'

'A Slinky!' Magorium said. 'It's a wonderful toy. Slinky! Fun for a girl or a boy!'

Very Close to the End . . .

WRIGHT BROTHERS

Magorium first met Wilbur and Orville Wright while buying a bicycle from them. He'd heard of their superior craftsmanship and had travelled to Dayton, Ohio, to see their handiwork with his own eyes at the Wright Cycle Shop. He bought their top-of-the-line Van Cleve model which was tall and sleek. When he signed his name on the cheque, Wilbur gasped. 'Magorium!' he said. 'You're the famous toy inventor!'

'Nice to meet you,' Magorium said.

Wilbur was thin and pale with dark eyebrows and keen eyes and a bald head. 'Orville!' Wilbur shouted to his brother. 'This is Edward Magorium!'

Though a mouthy prankster with his family and friends, Orville was shy in front of strangers. He had shiny dark hair and a fancy moustache. He could only glance at Magorium. 'How wonderful to meet you,' he said. 'What an honour.'

'Our mother was the inventor in our house. She handled all things mechanical and she even made us toys,' Wilbur said. 'We're inventors ourselves.'

'It's a supreme bicycle,' Magorium said, assuming that's what Wilbur was talking about. 'The most amazing I've ever seen.'

'Oh, no,' Wilbur said, leaning forward. 'We're trying to invent something bigger, much bigger, much bolder.'

'You are?' Magorium whispered. 'May I ask . . .'

'No, no,' Orville whispered urgently to his brother. 'Don't say it, Wilbur. It's embarrassing. Don't mention it. He won't believe us.'

'Won't believe you?' Magorium said. 'I specialize in believing the unbelievable! It's what I do best!'

The two brothers exchanged a look and then Orville nodded.

'We want to invent a flying machine,' Wilbur said.

Magorium reared back for a moment. He thought of himself as a boy at the Aviary window. He hadn't thought of it for ages – the tingling, the whirring, the breaking open of imagination. He felt it all again! He'd wanted to become a bird once upon a time. He'd wanted to fly. He felt a little dizzy, not sure what to do or say.

Orville filled the silence. 'We've only done a bit of well-digging so far. The practice gliders sometimes hit the sand so hard that they form a crater.'

'Well-digging,' Wilbur said. 'That's what we call it.'

Magorium could barely hear them. He was so entranced with the idea of a flying machine. Finally, he took a breath and said, 'A flying machine! I've always wanted to fly!' He wrapped his knuckles on the counter. 'Will you let me know when it's ready? I'd like a ride.'

'Of course!' Wilbur said.

'Surely,' Orville said.

And with a hearty wave, Magorium got on his Van Cleve bicycle and pedalled towards the front of the store. Wilbur ran ahead to open the door for him, and out he toddled down the street, waving and singing; and right before turning a corner, he pedalled hard, got a head of steam going. He then took both hands off the handlebars – which is not recommended – and reached his arms out like wings and flapped them joyfully at his sides.

Magorium waited for a correspondence from Wilbur and Orville Wright, but years passed by. By now, he knew that monumental inventions took a long time and that he would have to be patient.

And his patience paid off. One day, he got a note in the mail – and an invitation to join the Wright brothers at Kitty Hawk to witness a test flight.

'A test FLIGHT!' Magorium shouted, and flapped.

He met the Wright brothers on the stretch of beach designated in the invitation. It was December and cold. The ocean was churning and the winds were brisk. Magorium wore his heaviest long coat and a hat. When he appeared on the dune, Wilbur waved and shouted, 'We may just do it!'

'You will!' Magorium shouted back into the noisy tide, the gulls cawing overhead, dipping and swaying so easily.

The brothers tossed a coin to see who would go first. Wilbur won. He climbed into the cockpit. He revved the engine and started to roll forward. The Flyer jerked and the engine stalled. The Flyer smashed into the sand.

But, oddly enough, the brothers were excited. They knew that they were one step closer.

For the next few days, Magorium stayed on and helped the brothers repair the Flyer. They became good friends, working side by side by side.

On 17 December, they tried again. Magorium was there, helping them roll the Flyer out of the work shed and on to the sand. It was freezing cold with strong winds.

This time, Orville was in the cockpit. Magorium was in charge of the clock. It was 10:35 in the morning when the Flyer lurched forward, gathered some speed then lifted off the launching rail. Magorium drew in a deep breath and held it. The Flyer hovered and batted around a bit, drifting over the sand. Orville was flying! A human being was flying! Magorium's own heart felt as light and airy and winging as a bird's.

Finally the Flyer landed on the sand – having travelled forty metres for twelve seconds. Magorium hooted wildly. The small crowd clapped and cheered. When Orville hopped down on to the sand, his brother shook his hand, and they stood that way, shaking hands for a long time, astonished that they'd actually done it, and maybe almost afraid to let go.

They flew the Flyer many more times that day – once with Magorium in the cockpit, his hat popping off his head as the Flyer took off and, when it landed, Magorium had sand on his teeth from having smiled gleefully the whole way. That night, Edward couldn't sleep. He put his heavy coat on over his pyjamas and walked to the work shed to look at the Flyer. He stared at its huge wings, its tough nose, its sturdy bones. He circled it three times and then sat down on a chair next to a table, filled with notes and sketches. And then his eyes drifted to a basket sitting on the floor. The basket was cluttered with white pieces of angularly folded paper. He walked to the basket, picked up one of the tightly folded papers, and saw that it was a paper aeroplane – something that was, once upon a time, called Mr Magorium's Creased Contraption of Gossamer Aviation – but now belonged to the world.

X-Ray

Maybe it should be noted that Edward wasn't completely shocked that he'd had the chance to fly, because once when he was delirious with pain, a famous scientist told him that he would.

In 1919, Magorium broke his shin while playing dodge ball in Paris. Luckily, Marie Curie was nearby driving one of her mobile radiography units, called 'Petites Curies' and so she rode up to the spot and took an X-ray of Magorium's lower leg.

'Yes, it's broken,' she told him.

Magorium was dizzy with pain. He couldn't believe that it was Marie Curie, the famous scientist herself, who'd already won two Nobel Prizes. 'It's you!' he said, but then he looked again and he saw his own mother's face, Vlada Magorium, her wild hair wisping around her head, and how she used to play him tuba lullabies that were really bedtime stories. 'Tell me a story,' he said. 'A beautiful story.'

'I think science has great beauty,' Marie Curie said. 'Scientists in laboratories aren't only technicians. We are also children placed before natural phenomena, and it impresses us, each time, like a fairy tale.'

His eyes fluttered. He was about to pass out. He said, 'One day I'd like to fly.'

And she said with great authority, 'One day you will.'

And, as you all well know, one day, he did.

YO-YO

Haven't you learned enough already? Haven't I told you so many many things you never knew before? Of course I have! And now you want to know all about the yo-yo? Well, do a little research and then reimagine it for yourself. (Was Magorium friends with a man named Pedro Flores? Did they spend hours one-upping each other with yo-yo tricks? What do you think?)

ZEN

Like Magorium, the Dalai Lama likes to collect and repair wristwatches. Magorium and the Dalai Lama have spent many afternoons picking at the tiny inner mechanisms of wristwatches, holding them to their ears, waiting for their little heartbeats to kick in.

And, all the while, they talk about world religions. The Dalai Lama is interested in many things – exactly like Edward Magorium. So they discussed Tibetan Buddhism, Zen, 'what is the sound of one-hand clapping', motorcycle maintenance and pop-culture phenomena like NASCAR and disco dancing.

They agree on the joy of wristwatches; however, they disagree on NASCAR and disco. The Dalai

Lama just can't seem to comprehend their appeal, and, although Magorium admits that both have led to some bad fashion choices, he has to stick up for them, if only because he's found that the glinting disco ball and the churning round and round and round of fast cars can be very meditative.

EPILOGUE

AND NOW YOU ARE HERE

Bellini shut the enormous book with a thud. I'd been staring off into space quite dreamily, and the thud jerked me to attention.

'But, but . . . there's more,' I said. 'Isn't there?'

'Much, much more,' Bellini said. 'But you have to find your way back, don't you?'

I nodded. 'Mrs Tarblage,' I said to myself. I'd almost forgotten her and the Alton School for the Remarkably Giftless and how I'd been sprayed by a puddle and mixed up with a Japanese tour group. I'd been swept into the life of Edward Magorium. Time had passed. Not only my socks, but all of my clothes were dry. The rain had stopped. The afternoon sun was warming the streets. 'But what happened to Magorium? Where is he now?'

Bellini stood up and stretched, and then he nodded to me and said, 'Come along.'

We walked to a set of stairs in the far corner of the basement. They led to a door. Bellini opened the door and there stretched out before me was the most miraculous toy store that I'd ever seen. It was filled with magical things – a dizzying, floating, whizzing and singing array of toys – stacked high and far and wide.

Bellini led me to a far corner of the store and there, on a see-through water bed, filled with lively spinning fish, was a man, dressed in a light-blue suit, wearing a lovely pair of shoes, and he was sound asleep.

Bellini put a finger to his lips.

'Magorium?' I whispered.

He nodded.

And with that Magorium's eyes popped open and the water bed sprang a terrible leak. Water came rushing out of it, careening over the floorboards.

'It's the lobsters!' Magorium said with a start. 'I can't quite get the lobsters not to snap, even accidentally, and break the liner. And I was just starting to have a most excellent seafaring dream!'

Bellini was already down on his elbows with duct-tape, patching the hole in the water bed, and Magorium started pumping water back into the bed with a bicycle pump that read *Wright Cycle Shop* connected to a hose.

'And who are you?' Magorium asked.

'I'm N. E. Bode,' I said, sticking out my hand to have it shaken.

He pumped my hand in time with pumping the water back into the bed. 'You have the handshake of a gifted young writer,' Magorium said. 'One who needs just a bit of confidence.'

'I'm actually not gifted,' I explained to Magorium sheepishly. 'I attend the Alton School for the Remarkably Giftless.'

Magorium stopped pumping. He was shocked and appalled. 'I've never heard of such a thing! Giftless? Did you say giftless?'

I nodded.

'It's not even a real word. Did you know that?'

'No, I didn't,' I said. 'But that's just the kind of thing that I wouldn't know, because I am giftless.'

Magorium put both his hands over his ears. 'Don't say that word again, N. E. Bode! I won't hear of it! I know gifted when I see gifted and you are gifted.'

'Thank you,' I said.

'Don't thank me!' Magorium said. 'You have the gifts, yes, but you still have to wrap them up, put a bow on them and hand them to yourself.'

'I don't know if I know how to do that, sir. I'm not sure what my gifts look like or how to locate them or how to wrap them . . .'

'You'll know all of this in due time, N. E. Bode. Trust me.'

And then the front door opened up and a woman with sharp elbows bustled in, followed by a gaggle of children with stickers on their anoraks, carrying black umbrellas.

'Mrs Tarblage!' I said. 'There she is with all my classmates!' I turned to Bellini. 'Thank you for everything!'

'My pleasure,' Bellini said.

'And thank you, Mr Magorium!'

'You're the one with work to do, N. E. Bode.'

'I know,' I said joyfully. 'I know!' Finding my gifts and wrapping them up and giving them to myself sounded like hard and complicated and mysterious work, but I was looking forward to it.

I ran up to Mrs Tarblage. 'I'm here!' I said. 'I'm here!'

She turned to me and looked at me quite confused. 'Of course you're here, Bode. Where else would you be?'

'But, but, I was lost and now I'm found!'

'Lost in your thoughts again? Lost in the wilds of your imagination, no doubt! Come along, now. We only have a few moments in this store. I don't know how you kids talked me into this! I have a divorce to finalize, you know . . .' And here she began to murmur darkly to herself.

I joined the rest of the kids, tearing through the toy store, touching, poking, spinning, twirling.

And then Mrs Tarblage whistled through her teeth, our little signal, and we all lined up. I was the last in line. I hated to leave. Just as I was heading out the door, I gave a final wave to Magorium and Bellini. Magorium gave a distracted wave, as he seemed to be deep in conversation with a lobster. I also saw a girl, about my age, sit down on the bench of what must have been Magorium's full-colour piano. The little girl started to play a song, a beautiful song, one I'd never heard before. The air around the piano billowed with colour, and then she stopped, as if she didn't know the rest of the song. She simply froze.

And I heard Bellini ask the little girl her name.

'Mahoney,' the girl said.

'Do you want to hear a story or two?' he asked.

I don't know what Mahoney answered, but if I were to guess, I'd say she answered, 'Yes! Yes, I would!'

The door shut behind me, but I stole one more glance.

It was the most amazing store I'd ever seen and it still is . . . and as Edward Magorium would say: You have to believe it to see it!

ABOUT THE AUTHOR

N. E. Bode is the charming and elusive author of *The Anybodies*, *The Nobodies*, *The Somebodies*, as well as *The Slippery Map*, and a forthcoming novel that fully explains how the curse on the Boston Red Sox was finally broken. For fun and freebies, you can visit the website theanybodies.com.